Seducing Simon

By Maya Banks

A Samhain Publishing, Ltd. publication.

Samhain Publishing, Ltd.
2932 Ross Clark Circle, #384
Dothan, AL 36301
www.samhainpublishing.com

Seducing Simon
Copyright © 2006 by Maya Banks
Print ISBN: 1-59998-263-3
Digital ISBN: 1-59998-112-2
Cover by Scott Carpenter

First Samhain Publishing, Ltd. electronic publication: June 2006
First Samhain Publishing, Ltd. print publication: September 2006

Praise for Maya Bank's *Seducing Simon*

5 Angels! Recommended Read! "Okay I'm definitely reading more of Samhain books...**Maya Banks** has created two characters that shine throughout each page. It's hard to not fall in love with Toni and Simon, as well as the other two men in their lives... Definitely a recommended read. This book, *Seducing Simon*, is filled with friendship, passion, and most of all, a love that grows beyond just being friends." *Lena C, Fallen Angel Reviews*

4 Cups! "Ms. Banks has written a great love story full of conflict and emotion. I found myself at one point actually getting a little misty eyed. Watching these two in a platonic relationship that moves into a heated one is very hot. The difficulties they endure in getting together will have you spinning. This is a wonderful story definitely worth reading." *Candy Cay, Coffee Time Romance*

4 Kisses! "With its sweet and highly sheltered heroine that must face the consequences of foolish and unplanned actions, and a hero that is truly sweet at heart but also having the hard head of a mule, Ms Banks has come up with a sweet tale of love, sacrifice and following ones heart...*SEDUCING SIMON* comprises of a wonderful supporting cast of namely AJ and Mike who are infinitely intuitive, bringing balance to the main character as their sounding boards. If you're after sweet and innocent then this one is for you." *Jodie Boulter, Romance Divas*

"SEDUCING SIMON is a compelling look at love between friends and the emotional roller coaster that Toni experiences while trying to get Simon to see her as more than just a friend. Compound that with pregnancy hormones and you're in for a wild ride that will have you experiencing all of Toni's emotions throughout this book...Now I'm hoping for a follow up story for A.J. as well as Toni's co-conspirator on SEDUCING SIMON, Mike. He was kind enough to give Toni pointers on seduction techniques that had Simon drooling. Mike definitely needs a story too." *Chrissy Dionne, Romance Junkies*

Dedication

To Amy: We did what we set out to do. It wasn't always easy, the road was bumpy as hell, but what a fun ride. Thanks for sharing it with me.

Chapter One

The living room erupted in cheers as the wide receiver ran into the end zone. Toni Langston watched as her brother and their two roommates, A.J. Spinelli and Simon Andrews began high-fiving.

"Toni, why don't you come sit down. You're missing the game," Matt called out to his sister.

She smiled and shook her head. "I'm fine right where I am." She continued to watch from her perch on a barstool from the kitchen bar. The kitchen opened up into the living room, and from where she sat, she could just see over the three heads on the sofa.

The three were embroiled in the game as it wound down to half time. Matt lounged back in the sofa, his brown hair, the exact color as hers, flopping around his ears, screaming for a haircut. A.J., Mr. Greek God, the golden one, was busy stuffing popcorn into his mouth. His sun-streaked blond hair was spiked on top, hinting at the amount of mousse that went into his styling. And Simon the Serious sat forward on the sofa watching the TV intently as play resumed. His dark hair, not brown, but not quite black fell lazily across his forehead. He turned, saw her watching, and winked at her, his leaf-green eyes twinkling.

Sighing, she looked back down at the pad of paper she was writing on and chewed her lip in consternation. Beside the pad was the rental section of the classified ads. She fiddled with the pen she'd circled a few ads with, her heart not really into choosing which apartment suited her best.

The fact was she didn't want to move out of the home she'd shared with the guys for three years at all, and she couldn't really afford to. But she had to. And soon.

She shoved the paper under the nearby phone book when the guys got up and headed into the kitchen.

"The Texans blew a fourteen point lead," Simon said in disgust as he walked toward the guys' bathroom.

"Hey, Toni, you care if I use your bathroom?" A.J. asked as he ambled over. "Simon's got ours tied up."

She nodded, and he flashed her a sunny grin.

"Whatcha doing, sis?" Matt asked as he took another beer from the fridge. "Want one?"

She controlled the urge to puke and waved him off. He shrugged and popped his open, taking a long swig from it.

He came back over to stand by her and ruffled her hair. "You've been quiet today. Not interested in the game? You're usually over there screaming louder than anyone. Something bothering you?"

She took a deep breath, knowing she had to confront him sooner or later, and she'd rather do it when Simon and A.J weren't staring at her as well. "I'm going to move out."

He wouldn't have reacted more violently if she'd knocked him in the head. His brown eyes popped open and his mouth dropped. He set his beer down with a resounding thud. "You can't be serious. What's wrong? What happened?"

"Nothing's wrong. Nothing's happened," she said quietly. "It's just time for me to get my own place." She immediately regretted bringing up the topic. She'd expected resistance, but she hadn't bargained for Matt's vehemence. "Can we talk about it later?"

He stared hard, studying her. "Something is up," he said, ignoring her request. "You aren't telling me everything. I thought you were happy here. We decided together to let Simon and A.J move in when mom and dad died and left us the place. Do you regret doing it now?"

She closed her eyes. This was going to be more difficult than she thought. "You know I love you guys. I don't regret letting them room with us, but it's time that I got my own place. Spread my wings a bit. Time to prove I don't need you guys taking care of me all the time."

"Is that what this is about? Do you think we're overbearing? Because I can talk to the guys. We can lay off."

She smiled and laid a hand over his. "Yes, you're overbearing. You all are, and I love you for it. This isn't about you or the others. I just think it's time for me to get out on my own."

"I don't like it." He crossed his arms over his chest and set his lips in a firm line. "And you aren't telling me everything. I can see it in your eyes."

"What's going on?" Simon asked as he approached the bar.

Guiltily, she raised her eyes to see his concerned expression. She flushed and wished the floor could swallow her up about now. Of all people, she hadn't wanted him to know yet.

"She just told me she's moving out," Matt said in disbelief.

"Is that true?" Simon asked softly, boring into her with his intense green eyes. Eyes that left her feeling like she had no clothing on.

Another flush crept up her neck as she envisioned him naked, over her body, her hands gliding over his broad chest and bulging arms.

She nodded, unable to speak or meet his gaze.

"Why?"

She fidgeted on the stool, twisting her fingers in her long curls. "I think it's time I got my own place."

"You've said that already," Matt replied. "In fact, so far, that's the only reason you've given. Why is it so important that you have your own place?"

"Don't badger her," Simon reprimanded. "I'm sure she has a good reason." He turned back and looked expectantly at her. "We'd just like to hear it."

Think Toni, think. What could she say? Certainly not the truth. World War III would pale in comparison. She'd rather suffer through an entire hour's worth of lecturing from the three of them rather than tell them why she had to move out.

Because of her own stupidity, her relationship with the three people she cared most about was going to be forfeit. They'd lived together for three years. But they had been friends for a lot longer.

It seemed logical to invite Simon and A.J. to move in when her parents had died. The four had been inseparable ever since the guys were in high school. The guys had gone on to become firefighters and work in the small town of Cypress, Texas they'd all grown up in.

"Toni?" Simon's voice filtered into her thoughts.

She peeked up at him to see his concerned expression concentrated on her. Clearing her throat, she said, "I want to get my own place. Nothing personal."

"I don't see how we can't take it personally," he began. "It seems as if you want to get away from us. Have we done something to piss you off?"

With an inward groan, she buried her face in her hands. "Surely, you didn't think we'd live together forever. I mean you guys will want to get married and have a family. I'll want the same."

Her head came up at Simon's uttered "oh."

"I think I see what this is about."

"Well, do enlighten me," Matt complained. "Because I'm in the dark over here."

"I think what Toni is trying to say is she's ready to start looking for a serious relationship. Maybe get married and start a family. I guess it's pretty hard for her to do that with us three breathing down the neck of any guy she brings home."

"Is that true, Toni?" Matt asked.

"Uhm, well, yes, I suppose. I mean, I don't plan on getting married tomorrow, but I suppose I'll want to in the not so distant future." *Never mind that she couldn't have the one man she wanted.*

Matt didn't look convinced, but he didn't say anything more. Simon continued to study her until she was ready to fidget completely off her seat. Why did she get the impression he could see straight through her flimsily muttered excuses?

"Is there anything we can do to help?" he asked in a soft voice.

"Uh, no, not really. Well, I suppose you could help me move when the time comes." She flashed him her best smile in an attempt to squelch the nervousness she felt.

"You know we'll help."

"Yes, I know," she whispered.

She heard A.J shuffle back into the kitchen, and she turned in relief, thankful he was interrupting the tension. Her heart sank when she met with his expression. It was odd. He looked like he'd just eaten her attempt at meatloaf.

He stared at her with a deer-in-the-headlights look. Something akin to horror and confusion.

"What's your problem, A.J.?" Matt called out.

He continued to stare at Toni as he walked slowly over. He held his hand out, and Toni's stomach lurched, her heart jumping into her throat.

In his outstretched palm lay the early pregnancy test she'd taken the day before. The two lines were faded, but still very indicative of a positive result.

"What is this, Toni?" he finally asked.

Toni froze, but anger quickly surfaced in an effort to cover her dismay. "What the hell were you doing going through my trashcan?" She snatched the stick from him and clenched it in her fist.

A.J. blinked in surprise. "I wasn't digging in it. I dropped my watch and had to fish it out. I couldn't help but see the test."

Matt whose mouth was permanently rounded in an O of shock finally snapped his jaw shut. "Holy shit, Toni. Are you...are you *pregnant*?"

Simon took her hand in his much larger one and gently pried the test from her fingers. Matt and A.J. crowded around him as he examined it.

"What does two lines mean?" Matt demanded.

"It means she's pregnant," Simon said quietly, leveling a stare at Toni.

"Jesus! Why didn't you tell us, Toni?" Matt asked.

"Is this why you're moving out?" Simon asked, lifting her chin with his fingers in a gentle gesture that nearly had her in tears.

She nodded miserably.

"What the hell are you talking about?" A.J. demanded. "Who's moving out?"

"No one is," Matt growled.

"Who the hell knocked you up, Toni?" A.J asked. "Tell me so I can go kick his ass."

"Was it that geek who took you out a couple of months ago?" Matt asked.

Toni looked in bewilderment as the questions came from all directions. Then she did the only thing she knew would shut them up. She burst into tears.

Warm, strong arms wrapped around her and pulled her against the solid wall of a well-muscled chest. "You guys shut the hell up," Simon ordered. "You're upsetting her. We won't ever get any answers if you continue to interrogate her."

"Jesus, Matt, you made her cry," A.J. said in disgust.

"Me? I wasn't the one asking who knocked her up."

"Quiet!" Simon roared.

Toni closed her eyes and inhaled the comforting scent of Simon's T-shirt. God, he was strong, and everything that was wonderful about a man. She said a silent prayer he wouldn't let her go. Not just yet.

A gentle hand stroked her hair, which caused her tears to flow even harder. "Come here, sweetheart," Simon said, easing her off the stool and toward the living room.

He settled her on the couch and enfolded her in his arms. "Now, suppose you tell us what's going on."

She hiccupped and looked down. Matt and A.J crowded around the couch, looks of concern and confusion marring their handsome faces.

"You don't have to say who it is," he prompted.

"The hell she doesn't," A.J. began.

Simon silenced him with a look and turned back to Toni. "How about you start with why you want to move out, and why you didn't want to tell us."

"I wanted to move out because I didn't want you to know," she murmured.

"Why not?"

She looked at Simon in astonishment. "Why, so you could all badger me about who the father is? I'd rather forget the whole thing if you don't mind."

His expression became hard. "Did he hurt you, Toni?"

She gulped. This was not a conversation she wanted to be having. She glanced up at Matt and A.J. who looked like they were ready to go out and commit murder.

"Look. I made a mistake. I'd really rather not discuss it."

"Fair enough, but I don't think it's a good idea to move out." He cupped her chin and rubbed his thumb over her cheek. "You need us more now than ever. Moving into a place by yourself doesn't make sense. We'd all worry about you, and while it may be annoying, we all want to take care of you."

"Toni, I'm sorry I found the test. Well, I'm not sorry I found it. I just wish you would have told us," A.J. said.

"Have you been to the doctor yet?" Matt asked.

"No. I only found out yesterday."

"How far along are you, do you know?" A.J. asked.

Oh she knew exactly how far along she was. But she wasn't about to tell them that or *how* she knew. "I don't know exactly, but I figure maybe two months or so. Look guys, I'm not in the mood to do this right now. I have a headache."

"Take some Tylenol," Matt advised. "Oh, wait, you can't. Or can you?" He suddenly slapped his hand to his forehead. "Shit! I offered you a beer while ago."

Despite the seriousness of the situation, she laughed. "But I didn't accept it, silly. Listen. The best thing you can do for me is to chill out and quit acting like I sprouted a third head. This isn't at all how I wanted this to go down."

"No, you didn't intend to tell us at all," Simon spoke up beside her.

She turned her head to him, surprised to see a hint of hurt in his eyes. "That isn't true."

"It's what you said."

"Yes, but I wanted time to adjust to things on my own. Obviously I wouldn't have been able to keep it from you forever. I was just…scared."

Once again she found herself in his embrace. "We've looked out for you since you were a little kid, Toni. We all care a lot about you. You don't have to be afraid."

"He's right," A.J. said with a nod.

"So what's next?" Simon asked, stroking her hair comfortingly.

She sighed and pulled slightly away. "I suppose I need to make an appointment to see the doctor. Get a blood test. I mean there is a small possibility the first test is wrong."

"Do you want one of us to go with you?" A.J. asked.

She smiled. "No, I think I can handle it. Besides you guys start a twenty-four tomorrow."

"But you'll come by the station and let us know," Simon prompted.

"Yes, if you want me to, that is."

They all gave her a look that suggested she was crazy.

"Okay, okay. I'll come by as soon as I get out of the doctor's office. That is if I can even get an appointment that soon."

"Are you staying?" A.J. asked. His question hung in the air and Simon and Matt looked intently at her.

"I don't know," she admitted. "I hadn't thought beyond my initial panic."

"You don't need to worry about it now," Simon said firmly. Besides, if anyone moves, it will be me and A.J.. This is your house."

"No!" she exclaimed. "I wouldn't hear of it. I mean you guys have been here forever."

"We feel the same way about *you* moving," A.J. said softly.

"Thanks," she said warmly. "I love you guys."

Simon squeezed her to him. She got up awkwardly and headed back to the kitchen. "You guys are missing the second half. Go ahead and watch. I think I am going to go lie down for awhile."

"You okay?" Simon asked in concern.

"Yeah, I'm fine. Just got a lot of thinking to do." She ignored the worry in their eyes and walked to her bedroom, shutting the door behind her.

She leaned heavily on the door, her knees sagging underneath her. What a complete mess. She had the urge to dive under her covers and stay there for a week. Yeah, sure, she couldn't hide her pregnancy forever, but she'd hoped to buy some time to get her life in order before she told them about the baby.

Baby. She smoothed her hands over her still flat stomach. Tears welled in her eyes. She loved it already. Almost as much as she loved its father. But telling Simon she loved him, much less that he was the father of her baby, was out of the question.

Chapter Two

Toni slept in the next morning, knowing the guys had to be at the station by six forty-five for their shift. Usually, she'd get up and shoot the breeze with them before they left, but this morning she stayed in bed to avoid them.

When she heard them leave, she swung her legs over the side of the bed and tensed for the wave of nausea she'd come to expect. She reached into her nightstand drawer for the small package of crackers she'd put there the previous day. Taking small bites, she got up and headed for the bathroom.

At seven thirty, she got into her yellow Jeep Wrangler and headed for the veterinary practice across town. She'd worked as Doc Johnson's assistant for the last six years, since she'd come home after one year of college.

He was a kindly older man, very much a father figure after the death of her parents. She loved her job and loved living in her small town even more. It was where she'd lived all her life, and she couldn't envision that changing.

Things could get a little difficult when her stomach started bulging, though. The only problem with living in a town where everyone knew you was, well, everyone knew you.

She climbed out of her Jeep and threw on her lab coat before heading inside.

"Mornin', Toni," Marnie called as she opened the door.

"Mornin," she returned.

"Doc's waiting on you in back. We just got in a dog with a broken hip, and he's prepping it for surgery."

Toni nodded and walked through the door past the exam rooms and on to the surgery area. She scrubbed then entered the surgery where Doc Johnson was waiting.

"Mornin, Toni. Just in time. Come on over so I can get started."

An hour later, Toni washed up and walked back out to the reception desk. Thankful Marnie was on the other phone, she hastily looked up the number for the local obstetrician's office and dialed. After making an appointment to have blood drawn, she hung up and returned to work.

At one, she took her keys and headed out the door. A few minutes later, she had the glorious honor of peeing in a cup that wasn't large enough to spit in. Then the nurse took a blood sample. Toni was asked to wait a moment in the waiting room, so she went out and poured over a magazine.

She watched women in various stages of pregnancy walk in and out of the office, and she wondered what it would feel like to have a burgeoning stomach. To feel the baby kick within her. Have a bulge for her hand to rest on.

The nurse stuck her head into the lobby and called Toni back. Toni shot from her chair and followed the nurse back to a small desk.

"Your urine results were positive, Miss Langston. I'll phone your blood results to you tomorrow afternoon, but congratulations. It certainly appears you're pregnant. We'll check your HCG levels and make sure they're where they should be. Then we'll get you an appointment for your first check up in four weeks."

Toni murmured her thanks and left the office. Numbly she sat behind the wheel of her Jeep. Thankfully she didn't have to return to work today since Doc was taking the afternoon off. She wanted to go home and hide in her room, but instead, she instinctively drove toward the fire station.

God, what a mess she was in. Pregnant. Single. No way to tell the father without admitting what she had done. What a fool she'd been.

She clenched her hands around the steering wheel as she neared the station. She pulled into the small parking area and stopped next to Simon's extra cab Ford truck. To her surprise and a little dismay, he was getting out of his truck with lunch in hand.

He immediately walked over, setting the sacks on the hood of her jeep. "How did it go?"

The concern in his voice was nearly her undoing. "It went okay. I, uh, well, I'm definitely pregnant." Of all the ways she'd imagined telling the father of her baby she was pregnant, this wasn't one of them.

He pulled her into his arms and she rested her head on his chest, breathing deeply of the faint scent of his soap. "Are you okay with it?"

She drew away and smiled tremulously. "Yeah, I'm okay."

"Help me take in lunch to the guys? They're anxious to hear from you."

She took two of the bags and walked beside him through the garage and into the station. Inside the guys were lounging around the TV. She and Simon set the bags on the table, and the rest got up and ambled over to sit.

"Hey Toni," several of the guys called out as they rummaged through the bags for a hamburger.

She smiled and returned their greeting. She was pretty much a fixture around the station house. A regular Dalmatian. Good grief, now she was comparing herself to a dog.

Matt and A.J. sidled over to her side. "Well?" Matt whispered.

She nodded and A.J. put a hand to her back, rubbing up and down soothingly. "You okay?"

She nodded again and offered a smile.

"You wanna hang out here at the station tonight?" Matt asked. "We're going to watch a few movies later. Might beat being at the house alone."

"No, I've got things to do at home. I need some time alone anyway. I'll catch you guys tomorrow afternoon when I get off from work."

As she made for the door, Simon fell into step beside her. She looked up in surprise when he followed her out. "You sure you're going to be okay tonight? I know this has to have been a tough day for you."

Her heart lurched at the tenderness in his voice. "Yeah, I'll be fine. It's probably just as well you guys are working tonight. Don't think I'd make good company."

"I wish I could be home to hang out with you. We'll catch up tomorrow night, okay?"

She smiled and climbed into her Jeep. "Thanks, Simon."

"Take care," he said softly, closing her door.

Simon watched her drive off and slowly walked back inside the station. Finding out Toni was pregnant had been a huge shock. She'd been like a little sister for so long, it was hard to imagine her *doing* anything to get pregnant.

His heart wrenched when her sad face floated through his memory. He was used to her sparkling. She was never without a mischievous smile, her warm brown eyes full of laughter. The light smattering of freckles, almost invisible, sprinkled across her nose just added to her pixie-like appearance.

She was a small package, barely reaching his chest, but she was full of dynamite and had long kept him and the others in line. In their house, she towed the line, and you better walk it straight.

He grinned to himself. Yeah, she was cute and fun. His smile vanished. Someone had taken advantage of her, and now she was left holding the bag. Well, she wouldn't do it alone. She'd been there to help him through his disastrous break up with Starla, and he'd be damned if he didn't return the favor.

When he walked back in, Matt and A.J. were waiting. "What's up?" Matt demanded.

Simon raised an eyebrow. "Nada. Just making sure Toni was okay."

"And is she?" A.J. prompted.

"Yeah, I guess as good as she can be under the circumstances."

"So who's the guy?" Matt interjected.

Simon shrugged and A.J. blew out his breath in a puff.

"Could it be that teacher guy from the high school she went out with awhile back?" A.J. asked.

"Could be," Simon replied. "Though I can't imagine him coaxing Toni into bed."

"Shit. I don't like the idea of any guy coaxing her into bed then disappearing," Matt said with a frown.

"This shouldn't be too hard to figure out," A.J. mused. "It isn't like we don't know when she goes out."

"Yeah, but we were working a lot of OT several weeks ago, so who knows what was going on while we were at work. She was at the house by herself quite a bit."

"Hmmm, yeah, you're right," Matt muttered. "Damn, I'd like to get my hands on that son of a bitch."

"You and me both," Simon said grimly.

She dreamed about Simon. About his hands moving over her body. His strong arms holding her as he made love to her. The same dream that tormented her sleep since that fateful night two months ago. She woke up bathed in sweat…and longing.

Closing her eyes once more, she conjured up the memory of that night…

Toni sank onto the couch, her heart heavy. The knot in her throat had grown until it was difficult to breathe around it. Tears pricked her eyelids, but she held them at bay, determined not to give into the overwhelming despair she felt.

The man she loved, had loved forever, was asking another woman to marry him. Even now, they were probably reveling in the joy of their commitment.

She blinked furiously as the ache in her chest grew. Matt and A.J. were working, thank God. There was no one to witness her misery. Simon should be working too, but he'd taken the day off. This was one time she regretted the fact they were all roommates. She wanted nothing more than to bury herself away from Simon.

She hugged her legs to her chest then rested her chin between her knees. If only she'd done something, anything, to make Simon realize her feelings for him. She'd never even given things a chance to see what might blossom between them. And now she was too late.

A slamming door jerked her out of her wallow. Her feet thumped to the floor, and she whirled around to see Simon standing in the kitchen, fury blazing in his eyes.

She stood up, half in dread, half in hope. He should be ecstatic, not angry.

"Simon?"

His fist thumped on the bar as he slapped his keys down.

Toni stood across the room, unsure of whether she should approach him. She'd never seen him this angry.

"She was in bed with another man," Simon bit out.

Toni's mouth rounded to an O, and her breath escaped in a whoosh of surprise. She hurried forward, stopping in front of Simon. She reached a shaky hand to his arm.

"I'm sorry," she said softly.

How could she feel this much relief when Simon was obviously in so much pain? But her heart beat a hopeful rhythm.

He let out an angry sigh. She wrinkled her nose as the smell of alcohol reached her.

"Simon, have you been drinking?"

He grinned crookedly at her. "You could say that."

Before she could respond, he stumbled over to one of the cabinets and pulled down a bottle of Jim Beam and a juice glass.

He looked back at her and raised a glass in question. "Wanna join me?"

"Simon…"

"What?"

"Don't do this. She's not worth it."

He nodded his head. "I completely agree." He walked around the bar and headed into the living room, the bottle dangling from his fingertips.

He set both on the coffee table and poured a generous amount of the liquor into the glass.

Toni eased onto the couch beside him. As much as she didn't want him marrying another woman, his pain was nearly her undoing.

Simon drained the glass and plunked it back down, quickly pouring another round. His fingers clenched the glass as he brought it to his mouth, the tips white with the pressure he exerted.

"I went over there to surprise her, to ask her to marry me, and I find her fucking another man." He shook his head, his lips twisting into a snarl. "What an idiot I am."

"She's the idiot," Toni said through clenched teeth.

Simon quirked an eyebrow then his mouth relaxed into a smile. Some of the darkness receded from his green eyes. He reached out a hand to cup her cheek. "Thank you."

She worked to keep from nuzzling into his hand. "For what?"

"For being here," he said softly.

She edged closer still to him. She rubbed her cheek against his palm. How much had he had to drink already? He'd just consumed two large glasses of Jim Beam, and apart from the occasional beer, Simon wasn't a drinker.

He stared at her, his gaze slightly unfocused, but intently rested on her. She put her fingers out to touch his lips, wondering how he would react, wondering why she was being so bold.

His mouth felt full, sensuous against her touch. His hand fell away from her cheek, down to her shoulder then began a slow glide down her arm until his fingers met her hand.

Before her courage completely failed her, she leaned into him, slowly pulling her hand away from his lips until her mouth replaced her fingers.

There was a short, jerky intake of breath on his part as her lips tentatively moved over his. She pulled away and tried to gauge his reaction to her advances.

He reached out a hand and thumbed her lip. She tried to breathe in, but she felt a hitch, and it stuck in her throat. Her heart beat erratically against her chest.

She wanted more of him, more than just gentle kisses and a few innocent caresses. She'd waited so long for him to look at her the way he was looking at her right now.

Placing her hands on his broad chest, she pushed him back against the couch. She smoothed her fingers over his shoulders and down his muscular arms. She loved the feel of his strength, the raw power that exuded from him.

Not taking even a second to contemplate her actions, not *wanting* to back away from the conscious decision she'd made, she swung her leg over his lap, and straddled his legs.

She stared into his eyes as she pushed her hands underneath his T-shirt and began to shove it upward. She gained confidence when she saw his answering desire. As she pulled the shirt over his head and it fell free, Simon pulled her against him, his lips sliding hotly over hers.

She wrapped her arms around his neck and deepened their kiss, meeting his tongue in playful abandon. Her own shirt began to work itself higher as Simon's hands slid underneath to cup her bare breasts.

Her body sang at his touch. Desire hummed through her veins. How she loved this man. She wanted to show him, to tell him, to make him see the depth of her feelings in a way she never could before.

To her surprise, he stood, hauling her with him, holding her tightly against his chest. Cradling her in his strong arms, he walked toward his bedroom. He kicked open the door and shouldered his way in. He laid her down on the bed then backed far enough away from the edge to slip out of his jeans.

Toni rested on her elbow, taking in every inch of his gorgeous body as he rid himself of his clothing. She sucked in her breath when he pulled his briefs down and bared his straining erection.

Like a predator, he crawled onto the bed, need glittering in his eyes. He straddled her body and grinned wickedly down at her. He tugged at her shirt until it slipped over her head. Then with a flick of his fingers, her jeans came unbuttoned, and he began pulling them down her legs, leaving her only in her panties.

He bent and kissed the skin between her navel and the silky underwear. Goose bumps dotted her abdomen, and she shivered as his tongue moved upward and circled the shallow indention.

He hooked his thumbs in the thin band at her hips and slowly pulled downward. Soon she was completely naked. No matter how many times she'd fantasized about such a moment, her dreams had nothing on reality.

He hovered over her, and she wrapped her arms around him, pulling him down to her naked body. Heated flesh met hers, his hardness an erotic contrast to her softness. His hand twisted in her curly hair as he explored her mouth with his.

Need tightened every muscle in her body as he inserted his leg between her thighs. Their limbs tangled together, rubbing, then he nudged her legs further apart with his knee.

Every touch, every kiss, every caress was exquisitely gentle, as if she was the most precious thing in the world. Tears swam in her eyes, and her chest tightened so unbearably she found it hard to breathe.

She'd dreamed of him, of this moment for so long. Of loving him, touching him, showing him how good they could be together.

Her breath caught in her throat as he slid inside her. The brief moment of discomfort was so fleeting it barely registered on her radar. They fit perfectly, like they were made for each other.

He rose over her, holding her tightly as their sweat-slickened bodies moved in unison. His hands cupped her buttocks, then slid down to spread her thighs further. The tension in her belly grew until she knew she was on the edge of something truly wonderful.

His lips lowered to her neck, sucking, nipping at the tender flesh. She wrapped her arms around him as her orgasm rippled through her abdomen. She twisted and shuddered, and she gripped him even tighter.

"That's it, baby," he murmured against her ear.

He tensed above her and moaned low in his throat. She wrapped her legs around him as he surged more deeply into her. He expelled his breath in one long hiss before he relaxed and slowly sank down over her.

She sighed and snuggled deeper into his arms. He felt so good. Wrapped around her like he owned every inch of her.

"I love you," she whispered.

He shifted so that his weight settled to the side, and he wrapped an arm around her, pulling her against his chest.

"Starla," he mumbled.

Toni stiffened.

"I'm so glad you came back to me," he whispered.

Every hope, every dream came crashing around her. Humiliation replaced her earlier euphoria. She closed her eyes against the tears swimming in her vision. God, what a fool she was. What was she going to do when he realized she wasn't Starla? Could their friendship survive such an awful mistake?

She wiggled slightly until she was enough away to see he was sound asleep. She had to get out before she completely lost it. Carefully, she withdrew, sliding out of his embrace, praying he wouldn't wake up and see her naked in his bed. She tensed as he stirred, but he merely swung his arm over his head and resumed his even breathing.

She collected her clothes and ran for the door, bolting down the hall into the living room. Tears flooded her eyes, spilling down her cheeks. What was she going to do?

She yanked her pants on then pulled the shirt over her head. She wanted to scream, wanted to hurt someone as badly as she hurt right now.

She closed her eyes. *Stupid, stupid, stupid.*

She wilted on the couch, burying her face in her hands. What had been the most beautiful experience of her life now flopped in the final throes of a brutal death. And worse, she'd have to face Simon when he woke up and realized what a horrible mistake he'd made.

She sat there all night, dreading the morning when Simon would awaken to what they had done. She couldn't sleep, couldn't focus on anything but the moment he'd called her Starla.

Long after the first light of dawn peeked through the French doors leading to the deck, Toni heard the sound of Simon's door. She tensed as his footsteps shuffled along the carpeted hallway.

Anxiety settled in and began eating away at her insides.

He walked into the living room wearing shorts and a T-shirt, his hair rumpled and his face haggard. He looked like hell. Much like she felt.

"Hey," he said softly.

She swallowed, her mouth gone dry.

He padded over and sat down beside her, squeezing her knee with his hand.

"I just wanted to say thanks," he said.

She stared at him. Was he out of his mind? He was thanking her?

"I really appreciate you being there last night. You're a great friend."

Realization began to dawn, and her heart tripped and sped up. He didn't remember. It had to be the explanation. How else could he casually walk in as if nothing happened?

As much as the idea of him not even remembering making love to her stung, she was vastly relieved she'd been saved the humiliation of the whole messy ordeal.

She closed her eyes briefly, sadness mixing with the overwhelming relief. She had gone back to being the little sister, the best friend, anyone but the desirable woman she wanted him to see...

🚌 🚌 🚌

With a sigh, Toni gave up on sleep. The memory of that night burned too brightly in her mind. She crawled out of bed and headed for the shower. The guys would be getting off soon. As she sometimes did, she prepared breakfast for them and left it out for them to eat. After some dry toast, she locked up and left.

The morning was busy and passed in a blur. She took a quick lunch break and ate half a sandwich and some water. When she went back up front, Mrs. Hauffrey was waiting with her two poodles.

"Antonia, darling, how are you?"

"I'm fine, Mrs. Hauffrey. How are Fritz and Fifi?"

"Oh they're lovely. Just here for a check-up." Her gaze sharpened, her mammoth earrings dangling fiercely as she leaned forward. "Now darling, you know I'm not one to pry, but I saw you come out of the clinic yesterday and couldn't help but be concerned. Is everything all right?" Her eyes were wide, innocence etched on her heavily made up features. She even managed a look of concern.

Toni sighed. *Not one to pry, my ass.* The woman could pry a steel trap open with her teeth. Her eyes gleamed in excitement at the prospect of juicy gossip. Well Toni wasn't going to be fodder for the ladies group at the Baptist Church.

"Couldn't be better," Toni said with a smile. "If you'll bring the dogs back, Doc will see them now."

The look of disappointment on the older woman's face was priceless. She'd have enough to gossip about when Toni started showing. Which shouldn't be too far in the distant future.

Shortly after four, Toni saw the last scheduled appointment out the door and began closing up. Exhaustion permeated every pore in her body. It would be a miracle if she could stay awake enough to drive home.

She trudged out to the parking lot and slipped into the seat of her Jeep. God, it felt good to sit down. It had been a crazy day in the office, and breaks had been few and far between.

Fifteen minutes later, she pulled up to the house and turned off the ignition. All the guys were home judging by the trucks parked in the driveway. Why did she feel so awkward about facing them now? Taking a deep breath, she got out and trekked toward the door. She needed her bed in the worst way.

Matt and A.J. were watching TV, and Simon was in the kitchen cooking. She walked by with a small wave. Honestly, it was all she could muster. Speaking would have sapped whatever remaining energy she had left. She ignored Simon's inquisitive stare.

She didn't even bother undressing once she got to her room. She tossed her purse down and crawled into the covers.

"Toni? Everything okay?" Simon's voice reached her just as she felt him sit on the bed beside her.

"Tired." It was all she could manage.

His hand rubbed her back, and she moaned softly. "That feels good."

"Is she okay?" Matt asked from the door.

He and A.J. crowded into the room and stood beside the bed where Simon sat.

"I'm fine," she said, looking up at them. "Just exhausted."

"Should you go to the doctor?" A.J. asked.

"It's normal," Simon said.

"How would you know?" Matt demanded.

"I've been reading this." He held up a book. "I bought it for Toni. Has all you ever want to know about being pregnant in it. According to it, she will feel overwhelming fatigue in the early stages and it will taper off by the second trimester."

Toni looked at him in shock.

"I thought you might want to read it," he said smiling at her. "C'mon guys. Let's leave her to rest." He dropped the book beside her on the bed and bent over to drop a kiss on her forehead. "I'll call you when supper is ready."

"Thanks," she whispered.

When they left, she buried her head in the pillow once more. She couldn't do this. It was torture. Yes, she'd done something terrible, but even that didn't deserve such torment as this. Every gesture, every touch from Simon had her wanting, aching to curl herself into his arms and tell him she loved him. But now, she'd placed an insurmountable barrier between them.

She shoved the book aside and slapped a pillow over her head. How much different would this be if she and Simon were in a relationship? Simon would make such a wonderful father. They could have read pregnancy books together. Cuddle on the couch. His tendency to be overprotective would be endearing.

Her tears wet the sheets beneath her and she closed her eyes wearily. She wondered what the preggo book would have to say about her weepy fits.

🚌 🚌 🚌

A warm hand shook her awake, and she slowly climbed from the comfort of her dreams.

"It's time to eat," Simon whispered close to her ear.

She yawned broadly and lay there blinking at his face, so close to hers. It would be easy to wrap her arms around his neck and pull him to her lips.

He extended a hand to her and pulled her up to a sitting position.

"Thanks," she mumbled.

"I'll see you in a sec." He turned and eased out the door leaving her to temper her raging hormones.

She was going to have to get it together. She couldn't continue like this. Not only was she setting herself up for major disappointment, but if she didn't cool it, she could wreck the friendships of four people.

That had a sobering affect.

Smoothing her unruly hair, she padded into the kitchen where the guys already sat at the bar. Matt patted the stool beside him and she slid onto the seat.

"How you feeling?"

"Much better," she replied.

Simon set a plate in front of her, and she sniffed appreciatively. Her stomach growled in response, and she didn't spare any time digging into the baked chicken. For once, the thought of food didn't make her nauseous and she was going to take full advantage.

"The guys and I have been talking," Simon spoke up.

"Uh oh." She set her fork down and eyed them suspiciously. "Anytime a sentence begins with 'the guys and I have been talking,' it usually means you've hatched some hare-brained scheme, and it usually involves me."

They laughed.

"Well, it does involve you, but I don't think it's hare-brained," A.J. volunteered.

"Do tell."

"We don't want you to move out," Matt said.

Simon crossed his arms over his chest and nodded in agreement. "We've talked it over, and we want you to stay here where we can help out. You've been there for all three of us, and we aren't dropping the ball on you. Moving out right now doesn't make sense. We don't want you to have to go through this alone. Besides, this is your house."

Tears welled in her eyes.

"Ahh shit, Simon, she's going to cry again," A.J. said with a frown.

Matt quickly handed her a napkin.

"It's normal," Simon said matter-of-factly.

"Let me guess, you read it in the preggo book," A.J. said rolling his eyes.

"As a matter of fact, I did," he replied. "You can also expect her to be moody, prone to tears, easily fatigued, and nauseous for the first trimester."

"Gee thanks," Toni muttered. "Nothing like kicking a girl when she's down."

"The good news is that all changes with the second trimester. See, then—"

"Simon," Matt interrupted.

"What?"

"Shut up!"

He grinned. "Fascinating stuff. You should read it sometime."

"So will you stay?" A.J. asked, directing the attention back to Toni.

"Yeah, I'll stay," she replied. "For now, at least."

Chapter Three

Despite the fact she had been exhausted when she went to bed, Toni couldn't sleep. After tossing restlessly for an hour, she shoved aside the lacy covers and swung her feet to the floor. Running a hand through her hair, she sighed and got up.

She shuffled to the kitchen and poured herself a glass of juice. Then she tiptoed into the living room and sank into the couch with the remote. She turned the volume down low so she wouldn't wake the guys.

To her delight, *Lonesome Dove* was airing on a cable station, so she settled down to watch it. She'd been up an hour when she felt a kiss on the top of her head.

"Can't sleep?"

She turned at hearing Simon's voice to see him standing behind the couch in just a pair of boxers. He walked around and sat down beside her.

"Everything okay?" he asked.

"Yeah, couldn't sleep." And she hadn't a prayer of ever sleeping now. The muscles rippled across his bare chest as he sat back and stretched an arm over the back of the sofa. He propped his foot on his knee, giving her a great view of his tanned legs. Gulping, she quickly turned her attention back to the TV.

"Wanna talk?" he asked.

She glanced back over at him and let out her breath in a long shaky sigh. "Not really."

"Now why don't I believe that?"

"I'm just scared," she admitted. She never could resist him. He had a way of coaxing words from a mute.

"Come here," he said, gesturing for her to lean into his arms.

He pulled her to his chest, and she snuggled against him, loving the comfort of his embrace. "I won't tell you not to be scared. Heck, I'd be petrified, but the important thing is, you aren't alone. There isn't anything me or the others won't do for you. You helped me through a rough time in my life, and I am going to be here every step of the way through your pregnancy."

She turned her face into his chest and curled her arms around his neck. "Thanks, Simon. I don't know what I'd do without you." She hugged him fiercely, tears slipping down her cheeks as the stress of the past few days came rushing out.

He stroked her hair and hugged her just as tightly. When her sobs quieted, he pulled her away and wiped her tears with his thumb. "Feel better?"

She sniffed and shook her head.

"You know you can talk to me anytime."

"Yes, I know," she whispered. Except she couldn't. Not this time. And it made her want to cry harder.

"Want some more juice?"

She smiled. "Yeah, I'll take a glass."

He got up and went into the kitchen to pour her juice then returned to sit by her. He held out his arm for her to lay her head back on his chest, and the two turned their attention back to the TV.

"Simon?"

"Hmmm?"

"Do you think I screwed up?"

"No, sweetheart. Do you?"

"No. I don't regret it. It wasn't the right thing to do, but I don't regret it."

"That's all that matters then."

She snuggled back into his chest and closed her eyes. If he knew the truth, his answer would probably be different, but for now, it felt good to have his support.

"When do you go back to the doctor?"

"Not for a month."

"Want me to come with?"

She rose up and looked at him in surprise. "You'd do that?"

"Sure, if you don't want to go alone, that is."

"I'd like that." She smiled at him. "Thanks, Simon."

He winked at her. "No problem."

🚒 🚒 🚒

Simon opened his eyes and yawned widely. He looked down to see Toni still fast asleep on his chest. He smiled and gently eased from beneath her and placed a cushion under her head.

She looked so innocent in sleep. Just like the same Toni he'd known for years. Only she was pregnant. It was hard for him to comprehend. But then she *was* twenty-five years old. Not like she'd stay a bright-eyed eighteen-year-old forever.

He sauntered into the kitchen and opened the fridge. Taking out the ingredients for an omelet, he began preparing breakfast. A few minutes later, A.J. came stumbling in, bleary-eyed and looking like hell.

"Rough night?" Simon asked with a raised brow.

He grunted in response. "Hey, what's Toni doing on the couch?"

"Shhh, don't wake her. She couldn't sleep last night."

"You stay up with her?"

"Yeah, I just woke up."

A.J. frowned and looked at his watch. "She's gonna be late for work."

"I wasn't planning on waking her. She's exhausted. She needs the rest. The girl is completely stressed out. I was thinking about calling Doc Johnson and telling him she wouldn't be in today."

"Yeah, she looks like she could use the shut-eye. You fixin' breakfast?"

"For me, I am."

"Oh, come on, you know I can't cook for shit. Have a heart and make me an omelet."

Simon rolled his eyes, but good-naturedly complied.

"So did she tell you who the guy is?" A.J. asked around a mouthful of egg.

"We didn't discuss it."

"What *did* you talk about then?"

"Nosey this morning, aren't we?"

He shrugged. "Just curious. I'm as worried about her as you are."

"I offered to go to her appointments with her."

A.J.'s brow shot up. "Seriously?"

"You have a problem with it?"

"Nah, I just didn't picture you as the type to be caught dead in an office with a bunch of pregnant women."

"I'm doing it for Toni," he said evenly.

"Maybe you ought to consider hooking up with her."

Simon threw a dishtowel at him. "Get real."

"I can think of worse things. Starla comes to mind."

"Point taken, but Toni isn't like that. She deserves someone who can do a lot more for her than I can. Besides, she's *Toni*."

"Yeah, she is, but she's also one gorgeous chick, or hadn't you ever noticed? And she happens to be the most genuine woman I've ever met. When do you ever find those combined qualities in a girl?"

"What are you guys talking about?" Matt asked, rubbing his eyes sleepily.

"How hot your sister is," A.J said in an innocent voice.

Matt's eyes came open. "What?"

"Correction, A.J. is dithering on about how gorgeous she is."

"And you don't think she is?" Matt shot back.

"I am not having this conversation," Simon replied. Had they all lost their minds? Sure Toni was pretty, smart, fun. She had more integrity in her little finger than most people would ever have. She was loving, caring and loyal. *Everything you want in a woman.* And she'd never betray him like Starla had. But she was Toni. Kid sister Toni. Toni who trusted him.

Never mind how she'd felt in his arms. Or how he'd caught a glimpse of her small breasts through her thin T-shirt. The perfect size. Not too big, not too small, just enough to fill his hand. Any more was a waste.

He shook his head. Man, he needed to snap out of it. It wouldn't work. The timing sucked. Besides, she was pregnant with another man's child.

It shouldn't bother him that another man had made love to Toni, but it did. The urge to smash something suddenly became appealing.

"You gonna call Doc Johnson, or should I?" A.J's voice filtered through his thoughts.

"Why are you calling him?" Matt demanded.

"Be quiet or you'll wake Toni up," Simon said, pointing to the couch. "I'm calling to tell him she won't be in. She needs the rest."

"She's not going to like it," Matt advised. "She's never missed a day of work."

"Precisely why she needs to take one off," Simon replied. "She didn't sleep at all last night, and she's exhausted. I don't think she ought to go into work today."

"Suit yourself, but I'm not taking responsibility," Matt said with a grin.

After making the call, Simon started clearing away the dishes, but not before leaving enough stuff out to cook an omelet for Toni when she woke up. She'd already slept later than he'd ever known her to sleep.

On cue he saw her stir then stretch sleepily.

Slowly, Toni surfaced from the loveliest dream. She blinked lazily and snuggled back into the couch. The couch?

"Shit!" She scrambled up, nearly falling as she struggled to get out of the couch.

She hit the floor at a dead run, but Simon stuck out his arm and caught her as she dashed by.

"Slow it down and park it back on the couch. You're resting today."

"I'm late for work," she said struggling to get out of his grasp.

"You don't work today."

"Huh?"

"I called Doc Johnson and told him you wouldn't be in."

"You did what?" Her foggy brain fought to comprehend what he was saying.

"You needed the rest."

"You called and told them I wasn't coming in?"

"Ahh the birds finally pecked you on the head," he teased.

"Why didn't you wake me up so I could go in on time?"

"You were tired," he said quietly. "You need to rest. Take a day to figure things out."

Damn him and his logic. Simon the Serious struck again. Only he had a good point. It would feel good to take a day to rest. Maybe she'd feel better and not so unbelievably tired all the time.

"Want something to eat?" he asked, letting her go.

She wrinkled her nose. "Toast and juice?"

"I live to serve."

She glanced down at her tattered T-shirt and gym shorts. "Do I have time for a shower and change?"

"I'll dish it up in fifteen. Sound good?"

"Thanks," she said, stretching up to kiss him on the cheek.

She hurried to shower, eager to start her day of doing nothing. As much as she loved her job, a day off sounded next to Heaven. And Simon was right. She needed time to think about what she was going to do.

Minutes later, she pulled on a pair of shorts and an oversize T-shirt. She secured her hair in a clip at the base of her neck and went back into the kitchen to eat.

"Mornin' Toni," A.J. called from the living room.

"Hey, A.J. How was the date last night?"

He scowled at her, and she stifled a giggle. "That bad huh?"

"Hmm only if you consider a blind date with Attila the Hun's twin sister bad."

"Ouch. That's bad."

Simon set a plate of toast in front of her, and poured a tall glass of juice. "Eat up."

She ate with gusto. She was on her second piece when she suddenly regretted eating at all. Her stomach curled into a tight knot, and a fine sheen of sweat broke out on her forehead. Cautiously, she sipped at the juice, trying desperately to control the wave of nausea.

"You okay, Toni?" Simon's concerned voice echoed beside her.

She lunged from the stool and barreled into her bathroom. She just made it to the toilet before heaves racked her body. Placing her hands on the toilet seat, she leaned heavily on it for support as she rid her stomach of its contents.

A cool cloth pressed to her forehead, and a comforting hand rubbed her back as her body shuddered. "Take it easy," Simon murmured. "Deep breaths."

"Go away," she wailed. All she needed was Simon to witness her puking her guts up.

Strong arms held her up, smoothed her hair from her face. "I'm not going anywhere."

She leaned weakly against him, taking deep, steadying breaths. This sucked. Plain and simple. How mortifying to be puking all over a guy she wanted to notice her. Yeah he'd noticed all right.

"Better?"

She nodded and walked shakily over to the sink to wash her mouth out.

"I'll be in the kitchen. You want something to drink? Some hot tea maybe?"

She shook her head. "Nothing. I don't think I could stomach it."

He squeezed her shoulder and walked out.

She splashed cold water on her face and rinsed her mouth once more. Picking up the book Simon had bought for her, she walked back out of the bedroom and settled onto the couch beside A.J.

"You look like hell," he said sympathetically.

"Gee thanks." She punched him in the arm.

"I'll see you guys later," Matt called from the door. "I'm headed over to Stephanie's."

Toni waved. "Tell her I said hello."

Simon finished cleaning the kitchen then headed to the bathroom for a shower. Toni leaned back and opened the pregnancy book, but her eyes followed Simon's progress across the room.

A.J. put down the magazine he had been reading when Simon disappeared into his room. Feeling his gaze, she peered over at him. He was watching her intently. "Something wrong?" she asked.

"No, not at all. I was just wondering how long you've had a thing for Simon and why I've never seen it before now."

Chapter Four

Her heart nearly stopped. "W-what?" She quickly recovered and managed a look of scorn. "You've spent too much time in the sun, A.J."

He smiled knowingly. "Deny it all you want, but I've seen the way you look at him. And hey, if it's any consolation, I think you guys would be great together. He'd be a fool not to realize that."

"Your bias is appreciated, but c'mon, A.J., I'm not Simon's type."

"But maybe you should be."

She rolled her eyes. "You're forgetting one important aspect. I'm pregnant. I don't know of too many guys who want to date a girl who's pregnant."

His eyes softened. "Don't sell yourself short, Toni. Sure, there are guys who'd run screaming in the other direction, but there are a lot who'd care for you and your baby."

"You're sweet, A.J.," she said with a smile.

He gave her a troubled look. "What about the father? Does he know? Does he care?"

Her smile froze, and she looked down at her lap, avoiding his probing stare. "I don't want to talk about it."

"Did he hurt you, Toni?" His voice became steely, a thread of anger infusing his words.

"It's complicated," she mumbled. "Quit flexing your muscles, A.J. He doesn't know, and I plan to keep it that way."

His voice moved closer as he scooted across the sofa to sit next to her. "I'm so not understanding this. I know you well enough to know it isn't like you to just hop into bed with a guy. You must have cared about him. Problem is, I can't imagine who it could be. And if he didn't hurt you, why wouldn't you tell him? He deserves to know, don't you think?"

"It's none of your business," she said fiercely. She shot up off the couch and made a grab for her keys on the bar. She had to get out. She knew she was acting childishly, irrationally, but A.J.'s arguments were sound, and she knew he would drag it out of her if she stuck around.

"Toni, wait!"

She didn't stop to listen. She didn't have the answers to his questions. Couldn't afford to let him continue probing.

Simon toweled his hair and walked into the living room, his hands holding the towel around his neck. "What the hell is going on? Was that Toni leaving?"

"Yeah," A.J. said looking extremely guilty. Much like when he'd just eaten his or Matt's food at the station.

"What did you say to her?" he demanded. "If you've upset her, I'll kick your ass."

"I asked her about the father."

Simon swore under his breath. It wasn't anything he didn't want the answer to himself, but now wasn't the time to press her, and A.J. should have known it. "Will you ever learn to keep your big mouth shut?"

To A.J.'s credit, he looked contrite.

"Did you make her cry again?"

"Uh, no, I think she was more pissed."

"Damn it, A.J. This was supposed to be a day for her to rest and relax. Use your head for once."

He looked miserable. "Ah hell, I didn't mean to upset her."

Simon walked through the kitchen and looked out the front door. Her Jeep was gone. A.J. was well meaning, but could be a complete knuckle head sometime. Simon had an idea where she may have gone. If he knew her, she'd gone to the park. Her thinking spot since she was in junior high.

He headed back to his room and pulled on a pair of jeans and a T-shirt. He walked back by A.J. "I'll be back later."

As he continued on, a slow smile spread across A.J.'s face. He wasn't even going to ask what prompted that shit eating grin.

🚒 🚒 🚒

Toni sat on the playground swing watching the children play while their mothers watched. She would be one of those soon. Mother. The thought scared her to death. She wasn't ready to be responsible for another human being.

She loved children. Had always wanted at least four. But she'd also imagined she'd be married to the perfect guy. Live in the perfect house. They'd sit on the couch in the evening, and he'd hold her and feel the baby kick. They'd share their hopes and dreams of the future. But most of all they'd love each other, and they'd be happy.

A single tear trailed down her cheek, and she quickly bent her face into her shoulder to wipe it away. Her feet trailed aimlessly in the dust underneath the swing. How had she gotten herself into such an irrevocable mess?

She who had never done an irresponsible thing in her life. Quiet, shy Toni would never dream of seducing the guy she had a crush on for years. And especially not one who hadn't the capacity to realize what he was doing. He would die if he knew. *She* would die if he knew.

But on that night, she hadn't been able to hold back her feelings another moment. Angry at the woman who dared to hurt Simon, she had opened her arms to him determined to make him forget the pain. Determined to show him how she felt.

And God, it had been beautiful. It hadn't mattered that it was her first time. She knew instinctively that she would never experience anything like it again. It was what she'd waited for. He had worshipped her body just as she worshipped his. They'd spent the night loving until he'd fallen into a deep sleep.

She'd worked out the entire scene in her head. When he woke up, he would pull her into his arms and tell her how glad he was they'd found each other. They'd make love again.

Only when she *had* snuggled into his arms, he'd called her Starla.

She'd fled from his bed, her heart shattered into a million pieces. The hardest thing she'd ever had to do was to go on like it never happened. Accept his thanks the next morning for being such a good friend. Realizing he had no clue what they'd done. Then continue on, aching for him, wanting so badly for him to love her as much as she loved him.

And then she found out she was pregnant.

She traced circles in the dirt with her tennis shoe as she swayed back and forth on the swing. A shadow fell over her, and she heard someone sit in the swing next to her. "Nice day," Simon said in a nonchalant voice.

She turned her head up to see him staring ahead, watching the children play. "Did A.J. send you?" she asked with a sigh.

"No. The bonehead does feel bad though."

She smiled involuntarily.

"Now that's better. I haven't seen you smile in awhile."

She expelled her breath in a long sigh, her cheeks puffing out. "I'm not ready for this, Simon."

"Maybe not, but you'll be a wonderful mom."

"It's not just that."

"What is it then?"

"It wasn't supposed to happen like this." She struggled against the urge to cry. "I was supposed to find the perfect guy. Someone who was madly in love with me. We were to be married, then have children. We'd go to the appointments together. Get excited over the sonogram. Pick out baby furniture. Buy the perfect house."

She turned to look at him. "That's all gone now. Who's going to want to marry someone with a baby? I couldn't get a date before. I sure as hell won't get one now."

He looked stunned by her outburst. She looked away again. "It all sounds horribly selfish I know. I shouldn't be so self-absorbed now that there is a baby to consider, but I can't get over the resentment. And more than that, I can't get over being so angry at myself for screwing up everything I ever dreamed about."

"I had no idea you felt that way," he murmured. "I guess I never thought about you getting married and having kids. I always imagined you living in the same house with us and things never changing."

"Surely you weren't thinking that when you were dating Starla. I mean you wanted to marry her, didn't you?"

"No, I mean yes." He looked sheepish. "It's going to sound bad."

She cocked her head. "What?"

"I figured I'd move out, marry Starla, but that you guys would always be there for me to go back to, you know football games, weekend cook outs. God that makes me sound like an ass."

She laughed. "No it doesn't. I don't like the idea of things changing either." Her smiled faded. "But they will."

"Yeah, I guess so. Glad I didn't marry Starla though," he said with a wink.

"Me too," she whispered. If he only knew *how* relieved she was.

He reached out and took her hand, rubbing his thumb over her fingers. "It will get better, sweetheart. I'm sorry you're down right now. I can't imagine the uncertainty you must be feeling, but you aren't alone. Anytime you need to talk, day or night, or need a hug, I'm here, and I know Matt and A.J. feel the same."

Her heart constricted, and she bit her lip to keep from crying. Damn but she was a weepy mess lately. She'd never cried so much in her life. But damn it, she didn't want a hug. Not that she'd turn down any opportunity to be in his arms, but she wanted more. She wanted him to need her every bit as much as she needed him.

Simon wiped a tear from the corner of her eye with his thumb. "You want to take a walk? Or would you prefer to go back home?"

"Nothing exciting, but I think I'll head home and take a long nap. I'm tired. Tired of thinking." She smiled half-heartedly at him and slipped out of the swing. "I'll see you at home."

Simon watched as she trudged away. A.J. was right, she was beautiful. And not just on the outside. She had a beautiful heart. It made him ache to think of her hurting.

Honestly, he'd never given thought to pursuing anything more than a friendship with her. The mere thought scared the hell out of him. He frowned and rose from the swing. It wasn't as easy as asking her out. She was pregnant.

Running a hand through his hair, he strode back to his truck and slid into the seat. The annoying repetitive beeping of the open door encroached on his thoughts. He swung the door closed and rested his hands on the steering wheel.

He hated the idea of her dreams being dashed. Listening to her forlornly state the things she'd wanted twisted his gut. *Perfect life, perfect house, husband who loved her.*

He couldn't give her all that, could he? And more importantly would she want him to?

Painful memories of Starla's betrayal weighed on him. He'd been ready to commit. Take the plunge. He'd even bought a ring.

Finding her in bed with another man had given him an overdose of reality. One he hadn't relished. But it had given him a lot to think about. About the kind of woman he saw himself spending the rest of his life with.

Fact was, Toni embodied a whole lot of those traits. But he wasn't willing to risk a friendship that was extremely important to him. If it didn't work out, things may never be the same between them again, and that wasn't something he could stomach. Losing her was *not* an option.

The best thing he could do was remain a steady source of support. It could be dangerous to reach higher.

Chapter Five

"Do you miss Mom and Dad?" Toni asked Matt across the kitchen bar before she downed a prenatal vitamin with a glass of water.

He looked startled by the question, but his eyes saddened just a bit. He put down the mail he'd been sorting through. "Yeah, all the time."

"I really miss Mom right now."

"I bet you do," he said sympathetically.

"She always knew exactly what to do, and gave the greatest advice."

They grew silent for a long moment. "I miss her too," Matt said finally.

Toni set her glass in the sink and busied herself putting the dishes away from the dishwasher. Talk of her mother only brought home how blindly she was going into parenthood. Her mother wouldn't be here to guide her and offer support.

As if sensing her thoughts, Matt stood up and walked over to her, closing his hands over her shoulders. "You're not alone, Toni. I know I can't replace mom, but you can count on me for anything."

She turned and smiled, slipping her arms around him in a big bear hug. "And to think you used to torment me as a kid."

He laughed. "I guess I did. That is until Simon threatened to pound me if I didn't leave you alone."

"Yeah he did, didn't he," she murmured. She drew away and resumed unloading the dishwasher.

"Speaking of Simon, how was the appointment? He go with you?"

"Yeah, it was great. We heard the heartbeat. Doc thinks I'm about twelve weeks along. Gave me a March due date."

"You feeling better about it then?"

"I think so," she replied. And she did for the most part. She had spent the past few weeks numb to the reality that she was pregnant. But hearing the heartbeat today had brought home the fact she was carrying a tiny life inside her.

And already her jeans were too snug. She'd taken to wearing loose fitting slacks and sweatpants, but soon she'd have to buy maternity clothes.

"Oh, before I forget," Matt said, snapping his fingers. "Mike called for you awhile ago. I told him to call back this afternoon."

She frowned and leaned back against the sink. "What did he want?" The only Mike she knew was the Mike who worked for the fire department with Matt, A.J. and Simon.

"Dunno. He said he'd call back."

She shrugged and set her glass in the sink. After washing her hands, she walked to the French doors leading out to the deck and slipped outside. The sun was setting over the horizon, spreading an array of pink and purple hues across the western sky.

Settling into a lawn chair, she leaned back to enjoy the view from the elevated deck. As a song once lauded, there was nothing like Southern nights. The evenings were cooler with the coming autumn, and the faint smell of burning leaves filtered through her nose.

In six months her life would change forever. She no longer had only herself to look out for. Though she'd come to terms with her pregnancy, the idea of parenthood still scared the hell out of her. A lot of women seemed to have an innate sense of how to care for a child, but she wasn't one of them.

Her hand crept up to palm her abdomen. Only the slightest hint of a swell existed, and someone not familiar with her usually flat stomach would never be able to discern the gentle curvature.

A light breeze blew over her, lifting the strands of her hair and blowing them softly against her face. Maybe pregnancy was mellowing her, but she felt an inner peace she hadn't felt in many weeks.

The sound of the door sliding open pulled her from her silent reverie.

"Telephone for you, Toni," Matt said handing her the cordless phone. She took the receiver and Matt backed into the house.

"Hello?"

"Hey Toni. This is Mike. How you doing?"

"I'm good. How about you?"

"Doing great. Enjoying my day off. Hey, listen. I was calling because I wondered if you wanted to go out this weekend. Maybe catch dinner at Drake's."

An awkward silence ensued as Toni struggled with her surprise. "I uh." Shit. She didn't want to get into the whys and wherefores over the phone. No one at the station knew she was pregnant yet. "Sure," she finally said. "Sounds great."

"Hey great. I'll pick you up around six. That okay?"

"I'll see you then," Toni said. They said their goodbyes, and she punched the button, ending the call.

She leaned back in the chair and laid the phone in her lap. Her mind was whirling. Truthfully, she had no desire to go out with Mike, though he was a great guy. But on the other hand, it was high time she gave up her childish fantasies. Unrealistic dreams about a relationship with Simon and got on with her life. She had a child to consider, and despite the fact she couldn't have the one man she wanted, she didn't want to spend her life alone. Didn't want to raise her child alone.

Mike might not be the one, but he was a start. The beginning to putting Simon and her disastrous night with him behind her.

Today's appointment had been an exercise in bittersweet. Simon had gone with her, but his presence had been a painful reminder of what she would never have. Pretending was doing her no good. She felt like a dog being patted on the head, and it was getting harder to bear.

A few weeks ago such thoughts would have her in tears, but now she simply felt a deep seeded melancholy over the course, or non-course, her life was taking.

Well enough was enough. She swung her legs over the side of the chair and got up. She walked back inside to see Matt and A.J. sitting at the bar watching Simon cook dinner.

"What did Mike want?" Matt asked with ill-disguised curiosity.

"He asked me out," she returned nonchalantly. She crossed to the bar and replaced the phone on the charger then slid into a seat next to A.J.

Three sets of eyes turned on her. "What?" It was hard to distinguish who'd asked the question since all three of their mouths were open.

Simon stood frozen, spatula in the air. "Mike as in Mike from the station?"

"That's the one," she replied.

"What the hell is he doing asking you out?"

She pinned Simon with a frosty stare. "Could it be because he's interested?"

A.J. chuckled. "You stepped in it this time, dude."

"I didn't mean to imply that he wasn't interested," Simon said calmly. "I was surprised. I mean it came as kind of a shock."

"Why?"

Matt grinned. "You better shut up while you still have teeth."

Simon held his hands up in surrender. "Sorry. I didn't mean it like it sounded. I just had no idea."

"Nice to know Simon the Smooth has moments of stupidity," A.J. said with obvious glee. "For once it isn't me getting into trouble."

"I'm glad you all find this so amusing," she retorted. "Why is it hard for you to believe I have a date?" She turned and stalked to her room in disgust.

"Way to go," A.J. said shooting an amused glance at Simon.

Simon watched Toni stomp away to her room. He was still reeling from the news that Mike had asked her out. What the hell was he doing asking her out?

"If you frown any harder, something is going to go up in smoke," Matt piped up. "And if you don't flip those burgers, the kitchen's going to go up in smoke as well."

"You mean you guys aren't bothered by the fact Mike asked her out?"

A.J. raised an eyebrow. "Should we be?"

"Come on. Mike has a different woman every week. Do you really think we ought to be letting him take Toni out? You've heard him talk about how many times he's gotten laid."

Matt and A.J. exchanged amused glances, which only served to irritate him further. "What's wrong with you two? I'm being serious."

"Oh, yes, we can see," Matt chortled.

"Toni's a big girl. She's pregnant for Pete's sake. She's perfectly capable of taking care of herself. She knows all about Mike, and if she wants to go out with him, who are we to say anything?" A.J. pointed out.

Simon couldn't believe what he was hearing. Any other time the two of them would be growling like a pair of Pit Bulls if Toni was going out with the wrong guy.

He didn't like it. Didn't like it one bit. He turned back to the skillet and flipped over a burned hamburger patty. *That* one was going to be A.J.'s.

"I can't believe I let you talk me into this," A.J. said with a groan. "I gave up a date with Mindy Sue Stevens. I was assured of scoring too."

"Quit complaining and keep a look out," Simon snarled from behind his menu.

He edged the menu down and peered over the top across the restaurant where Toni and Mike were eating. So far they had appeared to talk, and Toni was picking at her meal. Why wasn't she eating? Was Mike bothering her?

The waitress stopped at their table temporarily obscuring Simon's view. He quickly ordered a dessert and waited impatiently as A.J. rattled off what he wanted to eat. When the waitress finally sashayed off, his eyes flitted back to Toni's table.

His eyes narrowed as he saw Mike's hand reaching across to cover Toni's. She smiled at him in return, but didn't make any effort to move her hand. This was not going as he'd envisioned.

"Looks like it's going well to me," A.J said with a shrug.

"Yeah, up until Mike tries to get her in the sack."

"Well, if that's where they end up, I am sure it will have been what Toni wanted."

"She's pregnant for Christ sake!"

"Lower your voice or we're going to be busted," A.J. warned. "Have you forgotten that getting in the sack is what got her pregnant to begin with?"

Simon gritted his teeth but lowered his voice to a loud whisper. "I can't believe you're so calm about this."

A.J. laughed. "You're worked up enough for both of us. Why should it bother you for Toni to move on and find someone? I mean, she's going to need someone. I can't imagine she wants to raise her baby alone."

"Yeah, but I don't see Mike as a likely candidate," Simon grumbled.

"Don't you think that should be up to Toni? Maybe you should step up to the plate," A.J. finished innocently.

He glared at A.J. across the table. This wasn't the first time A.J. had hinted he should ask Toni out. But it wouldn't work. If it was a disaster how would their friendship fare? And most of all, why would he be asking her out? Just to prevent her from making a mistake with someone else?

Or could it be he couldn't stand the thought of her with anyone else? Panic gripped his stomach. What a mess. He couldn't explain his sense of urgency where she was concerned, just as he couldn't make sense of his muddled feelings.

"Shit! They're coming this way," A.J. hissed.

They both lunged for their menus and flipped them open, sliding further down into the booth. Simon watched underneath as they walked by then scowled when he saw their entwined hands.

🚌 🚌 🚌

Toni slid into the passenger seat of Mike's truck and took a deep breath. The evening had been surprisingly pleasant, but she had to tell him. It wasn't fair not to let him know what he was in for. And where he stood.

"Want me to take you home now, or would you like to take a drive?" he asked as he started the engine.

"Is there somewhere we can talk? There's something I need to tell you."

He looked at her curiously. "Sure. Why don't we go get some ice cream and sit in the truck and eat it?"

She smiled at him. "Sounds good."

They stopped at the local ice cream parlor that had been in business since the fifties and got cones. They settled back into the truck and Mike rolled down the windows to let the evening breeze in.

He was handsome. Probably considered downright yummy by most women, and Toni was well aware of his playboy reputation. But she was pretty much ruined for any other man but Simon.

Mike slurped at his cone then ran a hand through his dirty blond hair. "So what's on your mind?" he asked, sitting back in the seat and resting his arm on the back. His fingers dangled inches from her shoulders.

She took a deep breath and looked earnestly at him. "I enjoyed tonight. I really did," she began.

"I hear a 'but' coming," he said with a smile.

"I'm pregnant," she said baldly.

"Isn't that supposed to come after we have sex?" he teased.

Despite herself, she laughed. "No, I mean I'm pregnant now. Three months pregnant. I just thought you should know. It isn't in most guys' dating plan to hook up with a pregnant woman." She twisted her fingers nervously around the ends of her hair.

"Whoa." His face reflected utter shock. He threw out the rest of his cone and focused his attention solely on her. "Wow. Really?"

She nodded.

"What about the father?"

"He isn't an issue," she muttered.

"Holy cow. Do Matt, A.J. and Simon know this?"

Again she nodded.

"And they haven't killed the guy yet?" He sounded incredulous.

"I haven't told them who it is."

He drummed his fingertips on the steering wheel. "Sooo, where does this leave us?"

"I guess you're more qualified to answer that," she said meeting his gaze evenly.

"Well I guess my first question is how do you feel about the father? From what I know of you, I can't picture you hopping into bed with him for the hell of it. Are you still hung up on him?"

She fought to keep her expression neutral, but she must have given it away because his face softened. "I'll take that as a yes."

She ducked her head. "Is it that obvious?"

"Yeah it is."

She puffed out her cheeks and expelled a long sigh, sliding down further into her seat. "This is hopeless."

"Is there no chance for you two?"

"It's complicated."

"Try me."

She jerked her eyes back to him. "Oh no, I know how you guys gossip at the station. No way I want this all over the fire department, much less get back to Matt, A.J. or Simon."

He frowned slightly. "I'd never say anything to the guys. Or anyone else for that matter. It might help to get it off your chest. It doesn't sound like you have anyone you can talk to."

She looked suspiciously at him.

He held two fingers up. "Scout's honor."

He wasn't the first person she'd choose to confide in, but he was right. She had no one else to talk to, and it would feel good to tell someone. Anyone.

"All right, but you tell anyone and I'll kill you."

A few minutes later Mike sat back in his seat, a stunned expression lighting his face. "Jesus, Toni. What a mess!"

"You're telling me," she muttered.

"And he has no idea you two had sex?"

"No. He thought I was Starla."

"Ouch," he said sympathetically.

"Yeah, ouch."

"How long have you carried a torch for him?"

"Oh pretty much forever," she said in a low voice.

"Damn. That sucks. Well if it makes you feel better, he is a damn fool. I know one thing. If you and I ever went to bed together, you can be sure I'd remember it."

She laughed when he winked at her. "Thanks, Mike. It did feel good to talk about it."

"No problem. And don't worry. I'd never say anything. I know we all tend to run off at the mouth at the station, but it's about non important things, you know?"

"Thanks. You're not a bad friend."

He sighed and keyed the ignition. "Well I guess that means I won't be getting lucky tonight," he said mournfully.

She punched him in the arm. "You're lucky I don't kick your ass for that remark."

He grinned. "You ready to go home? I wouldn't want to keep you out too late. If I know your roommates, they're waiting to pound me into the dirt."

"They won't have to. I might beat them to it." But she grinned over at him. "You know, you're not near as bad as Simon says you are."

He arched an eyebrow. "Don't be so sure of that, doll. I happen to like you more than most women, and then there's the little matter of three men who would cheerfully rearrange my face if I didn't walk a fine line with you."

"If you say so," she said innocently.

Chapter Six

"So how was the date?" A.J. asked as she walked into the kitchen and laid her purse down on the counter. He was standing close to the fridge in a pair of cutoff shorts and a T-shirt. Vintage A.J. fashion. And barefooted of course. She was convinced he should have been a west coast surfer.

"It was okay," she said with a shrug. She looked warily around, expecting Simon and Matt to appear any moment.

"Going to go out with him again?"

"Don't know. Maybe."

He leaned back against the cabinets and studied her. "You aren't very talkative tonight."

"It went okay. Really. I'm just a little tired. Where's everyone?" she asked changing the subject.

"Matt's over at Stephanie's and Simon is in his room."

"So why aren't you out on a date? Surely it isn't because of lack of interest," she teased. He was one guy who never had to look far for an interested party.

A peculiar look crossed his face. "I uh, well, I cancelled at the last minute."

She arched an eyebrow and gave him a mock look of shock. "You cancelled with Mindy Sue? The hottest chick to ever throw herself at the feet of the Adonis A.J?"

"Stop with the sarcasm already. I had other things to do."

"Oh, do tell."

"Nosey wench aren't you."

"Ahh, holding out on me. I'll remember that." She chunked a dishtowel at him, and moved past him into the living room. "I'm going out on the deck. Want to come?"

"I'll pass. Think I'm going to turn in early."

She gave him a small wave and pulled on the sliding door. Closing her eyes as the gentle breeze tugged at her hair, she eased into the patio chair and leaned back. She gazed up at the clear, starlit sky, picked the brightest and made a wish.

But wishing wasn't going to get her what she wanted. She needed to get Simon to notice her. As horribly ignorant of dating and the general act of getting a guy to fall at your feet she was, it wasn't likely going to happen without some serious guidance. Help. That was it!

The ringing phone interrupted her mulling, and she got up and went to the door. She saw Simon walking toward her room with the cordless phone and tapped on the glass to get his attention. He looked at her and waved the phone.

She let herself in and tried hard not to stare at his muscular frame clad only a pair of gym shorts. Even his bare feet looked sexy to her. His unruly hair curled damply at his neck attesting to a recent shower.

"It's Mike," he muttered, shoving the phone at her.

He turned and walked back to his room, leaving her to wonder about his odd mood.

She shrugged her shoulders and turned her attention to the phone. "Hey Mike. What's up?"

"Hey Toni, hope you haven't gone to bed yet."

"No, not at all, in fact I was just going to call you."

"Really? Was I that irresistible?"

She laughed. "Um sure, if it makes you feel better. I have a favor to ask, Mike. It may sound crazy, but I could really use your help."

"I start a forty-eight tomorrow morning, so why don't you come by the station around noon and we'll talk about it."

"Thanks. I'll see you then."

She hung up then stared at the phone in her hand for a long moment. "Or you could make a monumental fool yourself," she mumbled to herself. She set the phone on the bar. It was Simon's phone, but she didn't want to disturb him to return it. He didn't seem like he was in the best of moods tonight.

Well at least she wouldn't sit around tomorrow and be tortured by the sight of Simon. He and the others were off this weekend, so she'd be tripping over him the whole time.

Before she took two steps toward her room, the phone rang again. With an exasperated sigh she yanked it up and said hello.

"Is Simon there?"

Toni froze. She knew this voice. Was quite familiar with it. Starla. What the heck could she want?

"Just a minute," she mumbled. She should have lied and said he was out on a date and maybe the twit would back off.

She crossed the living room and walked down the hallway to Simon's room. Tapping lightly, she waited for his response. Any other time she would have opened the door and gone in. But that was before.

He opened the door, surprise written on his face as he saw her standing there. She shoved the phone at him. "For you."

She turned and walked back down the hallway, not wanting to hear any part of their conversation.

🚒 🚒 🚒

Toni stood in the kitchen throwing in all the ingredients for a crock pot soup when Simon sauntered in rubbing his eyes.

"Late night conversation?" she asked nonchalantly.

"Yeah, sorta."

"So what did she want?"

"Just wanted to talk," he replied, going to the refrigerator and taking the milk out.

He obviously wasn't going to tell her. She frowned and began picking up the mess she'd made. What could that nitwit have wanted? And why wouldn't

Simon tell her? They'd never withheld anything from one another. Well if you didn't count the fact she was pregnant with his child.

Suppressing her irritation and undying curiosity, she concentrated on cleaning the kitchen. She checked her watch and saw it was almost time to meet Mike at the station. She just had time for a shower and change then she'd pack the lunch she'd prepared and head out.

Twenty minutes later, she walked back into the kitchen and began packing the sandwiches into a small cooler.

"Where you going, Toni?" Matt called from the living room where he and the others were watching TV.

"To the station to see Mike."

She could have heard a pin drop in the ensuing silence.

"Date went that well?" Matt asked as all three turned around on the couch to look at her.

"I'm just going to bring lunch."

"Yeah, sure," A.J said with a grin. "And you said maybe when I asked if you'd see him again."

Simon watched her in silence a frown marring his handsome face. Finally he said, "Are you sure you know what you're doing?"

"This coming from a guy who was talking to his ex-girlfriend on the phone last night?" She arched an eyebrow. "The same girlfriend who cheated on you."

His eyes narrowed, but he didn't respond. She turned and walked out of the house, her keys jingling in her hand.

She drove the familiar route to the station house and parked beside Mike's truck. Collecting the small cooler, she walked to the door and stuck her head in. She was greeted by a chorus of hellos, and she waved in response.

Mike got up and hurried over. "Hey, how are you?"

"I'm good," she said with a smile. "I brought you a sandwich."

"Thanks. That was sweet."

She handed him the wrapped sandwiches and a bag of chips. She looked inquisitively at him as he dug into the food. "Is there a place we can talk privately?" she asked, placing emphasis on the word private.

He glanced around at the other occupants of the room then motioned her out into the garage where the fire trucks were parked. After wiping his mouth and swallowing the last bite of his sandwich, he looked back up at her. "What's up?"

She shifted uncomfortably. "Well, you know I'm in love with Simon."

He nodded.

"Well, uh, I want to try and get him to notice me. As something more than a friend. A sex kitten would be a step above the whole best friend/little sister thing," she said in disgust.

He gazed thoughtfully at her. "Well then you ought to go after him."

"If I knew how, I'd do it," she said dryly. "That's where you come in. I hope."

He stared inquisitively at her. "Me?"

She ducked her head in embarrassment. "This is humiliating. Look, Simon was the first guy I uh...well..."

"You're telling me he's the first guy you've ever slept with?" he asked gently.

She nodded, her cheeks flaming.

"And you have no experience in getting a guy to notice you."

"Right. I mean how many dates have you ever seen me go on," she muttered.

"So, you need to seduce him. Make him fall in love with you. But do it subtly. Make him see you as something other than a little sister."

Again she nodded. "If it's possible."

"You're hot, Toni. Show him that."

She looked at him in astonishment.

"I'm serious. Use what you have to your advantage. He already knows what an awesome heart you have. It's time to let him see what a hot chick you are."

"Have you been sniffing ammonia?"

He laughed. "Okay, here's what you do. Wear a white, thin T-shirt with no bra. It'll drive him nuts. Guaranteed. It'll work better than if you walked around naked. Guys love the subtle. The hint of the forbidden."

She gaped at him then burst into laughter. "Oh my God. I can't do that!"

"Sure you can. Here's what else. Buy one of those slinky camisole sets to sleep in and wear a robe over it, but let the robe fall open just enough to give him a glimpse."

"You are so bad."

"Wear a low cut shirt and lean over him. Touch him with your hand." He took her hand in his. "You have awesome hands. Small and dainty. The perfect size. Place one on his arm, his chest. Touch him when you talk to him. It'll drive him mad. You do all this and I guarantee he'll live with a hard on."

She burst into peals of laughter. "You kill me, Mike."

He gave her a wounded look. "I'm serious. Try it. I guarantee he'll notice. All of this is the lead up to the kiss."

"The kiss?"

"Yeah, the kiss. Torment him for a week or so then kiss him. Choose your moment and lay a good one on him. I'd bet a months pay he'll be putty in your hands."

Suddenly remembering Simon's phone call from Starla, her smiled faded.

"What's wrong?" Mike asked.

"I'm afraid it's too late. Starla is calling him again, and he clammed up when I asked him about it."

"Well then, you better get started. Seriously, girl. Don't let go without a fight. That's not the Toni I know."

She smiled again. "You're sweet."

"Wait until I have my next say before you decide whether I'm sweet," he warned.

"Oh?"

"I said all this because you and Simon belong together. He's the father of your baby. I know this isn't any of my business, but he deserves to know. I understand why you're afraid, even embarrassed, to tell him, but he has the right."

"I know," she murmured. "But I can't do it yet. I have to know if he cares for me independent of any obligation he has to the baby."

"Well he would be an idiot not to fall for you, and I don't think he's an idiot. But just in case, we'll throw in a few dates." He winked at her. "We can go baby clothes shopping or something, and it'll drive Simon bonkers."

"I don't know," she said doubtfully. "Do I want him to think I'm interested in someone else? I'd thought more along the lines of throwing myself at him." She grinned slightly at the thought.

He smiled indulgently at her. "It's obvious he takes you for granted. Not in a bad way, but let's face it. How many guys have you dated? He's got no competition. Fastest way for a guy to sit up and pay attention is for another guy to come sniffing around."

She chewed her bottom lip. *Would it work? It seemed so far-fetched.*

"What have you got to lose?" Mike asked staring pointedly at her.

She smiled ruefully. "Good point. Thanks, Mike. I'm going to think about everything you said." She stood on tiptoe and kissed him on the cheek. "I'll see you later. And thanks."

"You're welcome," he said with a smile. "Lord help Simon. I think he's going to need it."

She laughed and spun away, hurrying back to her Jeep.

A surge of excitement raced up her spine as she drove back home. Would her crazy plan work? Was Mike right in that Simon just needed to see her outside the role as best friend and little sister? The idea of him seeing her as a living breathing, lusty woman had merit. Provided she could pull it off.

There were only two problems. Well three actually. She didn't have a white T-shirt. She didn't have anything resembling a frilly camisole set. And she didn't own a robe. Hell she didn't even have any revealing shirts.

On a whim she turned her Jeep out of town and headed toward the neighboring city twenty miles away. Beaumont sported all the things Cypress didn't. Like a mall. A place to buy the things she'd need in her quest to seduce Simon.

An hour later, she walked out of the lingerie shop with a camisole nighty set and a matching satin robe. She then went into a nearby department store and purchased several new shirts and some maternity pants. She may as well make a full-blown shopping trip out of it since she needed the maternity clothes anyway.

She tried on two of the shirts and stared self-consciously into the dressing room mirror. They fit snugly over her breasts and flowed gently from the empire waist. The perfect shirt to highlight what little cleavage she had. And it served the dual purpose of a maternity shirt, so if the seduction failed, at least she'd get some use out of it.

She lugged all her purchases to the Jeep and checked her watch as she climbed in. Damn, she hoped someone had remembered the crock pot.

She pulled into the driveway at shortly after six and rummaged for her bags in the dark. Her hands full, she walked up the path to the front door and nudged the doorbell with her elbow.

Second later the door opened and Simon hastily took the bags from her arms. "You shouldn't be carrying all of that," he reprimanded.

"It's just clothes," she said in amusement.

"Want me to put them on your bed?" he asked as they walked into the house.

"Yeah, thanks."

"Hey, she's back," Matt declared as she entered the living room.

"One would think I never leave," she said dryly.

"And how was Mike?" A.J. asked innocently.

"Just fine. I'm sure he appreciates your concern."

He laughed. "Damn girl, you're on fire today."

"You guys eat already?" she asked.

"No, we were waiting for you."

"What's the occasion?" she asked suspiciously. She stared between Matt and A.J. Then realization dawned. "It won't work. I am not spilling my guts about Mike so forget it. There's nothing to tell."

"Gee, are we that transparent?" Matt asked in disgust.

"Yes, you are."

Simon returned and began taking out bowls. Toni stirred the soup in the crock pot and began ladling out portions in the bowls. Simon passed one to Matt and A.J. then took his own bowl and sat down next to them.

She sat down next and concentrated on eating the soup, determined to ignore their curious looks.

Finally Simon broke the awkward silence. "You guys still going to the car show tomorrow?"

"Yeah," Matt replied. "A.J. and I are leaving at seven."

"The one in Houston?" Toni asked.

"Yup."

She gulped nervously. If Matt and A.J were going to be gone all day then it would be a perfect time to try her hand at Mike's suggestions. Provided Simon was even going to be around.

"You not going with them?" she asked Simon casually.

"No. I thought I'd hang out around the house. Play some computer games."

Her heart fluttered rapidly in her chest. She lowered her gaze to the soup and spooned it up almost robotically. He was going to be home. All day. A whole day to make him notice her. It sounded so simple, yet so impossible

Well, one thing was for certain. She was going to get to try out her new sleepwear a lot sooner than she'd expected.

Chapter Seven

Toni woke early the next morning. She waited until she heard A.J. and Matt leave then surveyed her appearance in the mirror. The satin shorts and camisole actually looked *sexy* on her. Well, at least she thought they did.

She ran her hand over her stomach feeling the slightest hint of the swell that was slowly burgeoning. In a few more weeks she'd have a bonafide pooch. Better to do the seducing now.

She pulled on the satin knee-length robe and tied it loosely around her waist. Then she arranged the lapels so they bared about a four inch strip of the nighty. A flush suffused her face as she looked back into the mirror and saw that the peaks of her breasts were clearly outlined. One thing about pregnancy, her nipples were taut and stiff on a twenty-four hour basis now.

"You can do this," she said firmly to her reflection. "It's time Simon saw you as something more than a comfortable friend. It's time he saw you for a sexy, desirable woman."

With a determined nod, she turned from the mirror and went over to the door. She placed her hand on the knob and took a deep breath. Let the operation commence.

She walked into the kitchen, thankful for once that her room was on the opposite side of the house from the other three bedrooms. She'd taken her parents room while the guys had taken up residence in the three bedrooms that had served as hers and Matt's bedrooms when they were kids.

The setup had worked well. She had her own bathroom while the guys shared a bathroom on their end of the house. The living room and kitchen separated them. There was a formal dining room as well, but it had been turned into a computer room since they always ate at the bar.

She could hear Simon on the computer and wondered if she should venture in there or wait for him to come into the kitchen. Finally she decided to go to the door and ask him if he'd eaten breakfast. If not she'd cook and lure him into the kitchen. But first she'd give him a taste of her outfit.

With a grin, she walked to the computer room and cleared her throat at the doorway. "Good morning."

"Morning," he mumbled, not taking his eyes from the computer screen.

"Had breakfast yet?" She put one arm against the doorframe in what she hoped was a sexy pose.

He finally glanced up. "No." He turned back to the computer then jerked his head back up, his eyes widening in surprise. "Uh no."

His gaze was riveted on her, and she fought against the urge to blush and smile triumphantly all at the same time.

"I'm cooking if you want to eat." She slowly dropped her arm and turned to walk back into the kitchen.

He followed right behind her and sat down at the bar. She began taking out the skillet and the ingredients for pancakes. She felt his gaze on her the entire time, but when she would look up at him, he'd immediately look down or away. Anywhere but at her.

As she mixed the batter with a large wooden spoon, the motion loosened her robe and it fell completely open baring the plunging neckline of her camisole. Acting as if nothing out of the ordinary had happened, she set about pouring the batter into the skillet then leaned back against the counter to wait.

"So why didn't you go to the car show with Matt and A.J.?"

"Not my thing," he said barely meeting her eyes.

"What's your schedule this week?" It was an innocent enough question, but she wanted to be sure and plan for the days he'd be home.

"Twenty-four Monday, off Tuesday, and forty-eight starting Wednesday. Off Friday and Saturday and a twenty-four Sunday."

So she had today and tomorrow to make an impression then she'd have one day out of three where she'd see him a few hours in the evening. Might be good for him to stew for a while.

She turned and flipped the pancakes then settled her attention back on Simon. Her tongue felt tied. She'd never had any problem talking to him, but at the moment she felt as awkward as a girl on her first date.

When the pancakes were done, she stacked them on a plate and set it in front of Simon. He stood up and got utensils for them then retrieved the butter and syrup from the fridge. She poured glasses of milk then settled onto the barstool across from the bar from him. After all, he wouldn't be able to see her chest if she sat beside him.

An awkward silence ensued as they ate their breakfast. From time to time she felt his gaze on her, but didn't look up. When they'd finished he walked around and collected her plate. "I'll wash up, you go get dressed."

She nearly laughed at his directive. So she was getting under his skin a bit. Maybe he wasn't as immune to her as she thought. Remembering the other part of Mike's advice, she placed her fingertips lightly on his arm. "Thanks, Simon."

He flinched and drew away, piling the dishes into the sink. With a secret smile, she breezed into her room for part two of her seduction plan.

Choosing a pair of sweatpants to go with her sheer white T-shirt, she discarded her nightclothes and pulled the shirt over her head. But when she looked in the mirror, she nearly changed her mind. The dark imprint of her nipples was clearly outlined against the shirt. But he'd definitely notice.

She shuffled back into the living room grateful at least she was comfortable in the sweats and T-shirt. Perfect lounging clothes. And if they happened to make Simon squirm just a bit, all the better.

Simon was still in the kitchen washing up the breakfast dishes so she decided to wander in and get a glass of juice. She watched Simon out of the corner of her eye. When he caught sight of her shirt, he did a double take. He quickly glanced away, but his eyes kept drifting back.

Hiding her smile in her glass, she tilted it back, thrusting out her chest as she drained the juice. She set the glass in the sink and walked back into the living room. "Want to see what's on TV?" she called back to Simon.

"No, uh, that's okay. I think I'm going to go play some more games."

Simon walked into the computer room, frantically pulling on his collar. It was damn hot in the house. He switched the ceiling fan on, desperate for some cool air.

She was driving him crazy. When the hell had she gotten so damn sexy? The satin nighty had been torture enough, but the T-shirt that clearly outlined her perfect breasts was just too much.

Pregnancy had been good to her so far. She'd definitely filled out in all the right places. The dusky imprint of her rosy nipples had him dying to get his hands and mouth on them.

He was having insane urges to sweep her into the nearest bed and make some serious love to her. He was losing it. This was Toni, not some cheap lay. But here he sat fantasizing about kissing her in the most interesting places.

Lately he'd been having the oddest dreams about her. In his bed, writhing beneath him. It was so real he could almost taste her sweet skin, and somehow he just knew she'd taste of honeysuckle. He could feel himself inside her, instinctively knew just how she'd feel. The images bombarded him constantly. Her naked in his bed.

Oh yeah, he was falling apart. He needed to get laid. But for the moment the only woman he could picture in his bed was Toni. And that scared him to death.

The distant sound of the phone ringing broke into his vivid fantasies. A few seconds later, Toni appeared in the doorway holding out the phone to him. A frown on her face and those perfect, delectable breasts molded to every contour of that T-shirt.

"It's Starla," she muttered, as he took the phone from her.

He chanced one last glance at her chest before she turned and stalked out. *Wonder what was eating her.* He sure as hell knew what was eating him.

🚌 🚌 🚌

Sunday morning Toni got up and put on a pair of her new stretch waist maternity jeans and one of the tops she'd bought. Whether it had been bought to gain Simon's notice or not, she loved the way it fit. It hugged her breasts and outlined their curves then flowed gently from underneath the swells. If it was a little lower cut than her normal attire she wasn't complaining.

After yesterday's phone call for Simon from Starla, she wasn't feeling nearly as confidant anyway. But she wasn't throwing in the towel. Not yet.

Feeling confident she looked her best and maybe even a little sexy, she walked out of her room ready to take on the world. Or at least a six foot-two hunky fireman.

A series of whistles rent the air as she entered the living room where the guys were watching the football pre-game show on TV. Smiling, she struck a fake pose. "You like?"

"Damn, woman. Come here and give daddy a kiss," A.J. teased.

She burst out laughing and blew him one instead.

"You look great," Matt complimented. "I like the new stuff."

She looked pointedly at Simon who looked very much like he'd swallowed his tongue. "Well?" she asked him.

"You look nice," he mumbled.

"Nice? Hell, she looks hot," A.J. spoke up.

Simon scowled and turned his attention back to the TV.

Feeling very pleased with herself, she grabbed a bottle of water from the fridge and inserted herself on the couch between Simon and A.J. to watch the game. She made great effort to lean over Simon and reach into the chip bag he held. Finally he handed it to her mumbling something about not wanting any more.

She leaned back, munching calmly on the chips she held. She nearly laughed aloud when Simon suddenly got up from the sofa and left the room.

"What's wrong with him?" Matt asked in a bored voice.

She shrugged and glanced over at A.J. who was looking at her in amusement. She arched an eyebrow and looked questioningly at him as if to ask what he was finding so funny.

He emitted a low chuckle and turned back to the TV. "I think Simon may have met his match," he murmured in a voice only Toni could hear.

"Yeah, Starla's a real bitch," Toni said, being deliberately obtuse.

He snickered and swung a cushion at her. "You're evil, woman. Pure evil."

She only hoped Simon was taking a cold shower and her efforts weren't for naught. Tomorrow he was working, and Tuesday was the only other day until Friday that she'd get to work her wiles on him.

She watched the remainder of the game with Matt and A.J. hoping Simon would reappear, but he stayed in his room. Not willing to spend her entire day waiting on him, she decided to take her and her new look out shopping. Her confidence was at an all time high, and damn it, she knew she looked good.

🚌 🚌 🚌

"What's eating you, man?" A.J. asked Simon as they pulled off their gear after a fire call.

Simon wiped the sweat from his brow. "Don't know what you're talking about."

"Yeah, sure. You haven't been avoiding Toni like she's a hooker with the clap."

Simon shot him a dirty look and continued pulling his heavy jacket off. "Back off."

A.J. laughed. "Getting under your skin, huh?"

"I have no idea what you're talking about."

"Hmmm is that all you can say?"

Another wave of irritation gripped Simon. "Look. I don't know what point you're trying to make. I'm not avoiding Toni. She's not getting under my skin. I could care less what she wears."

A.J. dissolved into peals of laughter. "Oh man, have you got it bad. Who said anything about what she's been wearing?"

Simon leveled a glare at his obnoxious friend. "Shut the hell up."

"Well at least I know you aren't dead now," he chortled.

Simon sighed long-sufferingly. His head was beginning to ache, and the last thing he needed was A.J. harping on how sexy Toni was looking lately. Even if she was driving his libido into overdrive.

He got up from the bench and threw his jacket over his locker. "I'm going to go grab a shower."

"A cold one?" A.J. asked innocently.

Simon ignored him and walked out of the locker room, A.J.'s laughter ringing in his ears.

He nearly groaned aloud when he stepped from the showers and met up with Mike in the locker room.

"Hey, dude," Mike called out.

"Hey," he said without enthusiasm.

"How's it going?"

"Fine."

Mike studied him a moment. "You aren't very talkative today."

Simon shrugged. He was plagued by irritation at the very sight of Mike, and the only explanation he could offer was because Toni had gone out with him. Not an answer he was happy with. Why should he care who Toni went out with?

Mike grinned. "Say hi to Toni for me, will ya? Tell her I'll call her when I get the chance."

"Why are you so interested in Toni all of a sudden anyway?" Simon demanded, staring holes through him.

Mike raised an eyebrow. "What red-blooded man wouldn't be? She's the bomb."

Hoping Toni would forgive him for imparting her news, he decided to say the one thing he knew would scare Mike away. "She's pregnant."

"I know," Mike said calmly.

He knew? She'd told him? He frowned and looked away. And he was still interested? He glanced back at Mike who was wearing a serene expression. "What the hell is your game, Mike?"

"What do you mean?"

"Don't act all innocent with me. I know you too well for that. Pregnant women are definitely not your thing. For that matter, women like Toni aren't your thing."

"Maybe my thing has changed. That ever occur to you?"

"Stay away from her," Simon growled. "You'll only hurt her."

"Don't you think it should be her decision who she hangs with?"

"If you don't stay away from her I'll rearrange that pretty face of yours."

To his surprise, Mike chuckled then turned and exited the locker room.

Chapter Eight

Tuesday morning, Toni got up bright and early to get ready for work. She dressed with care in one of her new tops and went into the kitchen to fix breakfast for the guys who would be coming home shortly. She wanted to get into Simon's head first thing this morning because she wouldn't see him again until the evening.

She hummed as she poked around the kitchen, keeping a close watch on the clock the entire time. Maybe this second trimester stuff she'd read about was true. She certainly felt like a new woman. And she was positively glowing. Her skin was radiant, her curves softer, and her breasts, to her delight, had graduated an entire cup size. Of course moving from a B to a C was no huge feat, but it was progress. She suddenly frowned, wondering if she'd have to give them back after she gave birth.

The front door rattled then opened as she heard the guys come in. Matt was first through the kitchen doorway. "Smells good, sis."

A.J. and Simon came in close behind, and Simon scooted to the far end of the kitchen, sliding into the barstool that was the farthest away from Toni.

"Rough night?" she asked to no one in particular. "Simon looks like hell."

His gaze shot up, and he frowned.

"He was a grumpy Gus the entire shift," Matt said with a shrug.

"Well, here's your breakfast. I have to leave or I'll be late for work. I'll see you guys this afternoon." She set out the platter of eggs, biscuits and bacon on the bar and blew them a kiss. She made a point of leaning over in Simon's direction one last time before backing out of the kitchen.

She slid behind the wheel of her Jeep and took a deep breath. Today marked the first time she wore maternity clothes in public. While she in no way carried an obvious bulge in front of her, the shirt was unmistakably for a pregnant woman.

Small town talk would filter through the community of Cypress like an out of control fire. Before sundown, she'd be relegated to fallen woman, brazen hussy, and that "poor girl."

Thank goodness she'd already told Doc Johnson so she could at least be at ease with him and Marnie. The patients would be another matter unfortunately.

When she glanced over the schedule for the morning she groaned aloud.

"What's wrong?" Marnie asked.

Toni slumped in the chair behind the reception desk and held a finger to her head in a mock pistol style.

The older woman laughed. "It can't be that bad."

Toni flipped the schedule toward her.

Marnie took the paper and quickly scanned over it. "Oh. Dear."

"Yeah. Of all days to wear my maternity clothes. It just had to be when Mrs. Hauffrey had an appointment for her poodles' check up."

Marnie gave her a sympathetic look. "Want me to man the front when it's time for her to come in so you can hide out in the back?"

She sighed deeply. "No, I may as well get it over with. I knew when I left this morning that I'd be all over town by tonight. This will just facilitate things a bit."

Marnie smiled and patted her shoulder as she walked past with a stack of papers to file.

Toni twirled on the swivel chair, closing her eyes in disgust. When she heard the door open, she opened one eye and made contact with Mrs. Hauffrey.

"Good morning, Antonia," she sang out.

Toni gritted her teeth. Mrs. Hauffrey was the only person who insisted on calling her by her full name. Even her mother had given up by the time Toni reached Junior High.

"Good morning," she said in resignation.

She hopped off the chair and reached over to scratch the ears of Fritz and Fifi. She was rewarded by a lick from each.

"If you'll have a seat, I'll go tell Doc you're here."

As Toni turned, Mrs. Hauffrey let out a gasp. "Antonia! Dear, are you pregnant?"

She froze and rolled her eyes heavenward. Slowly, she turned back to face the excited gleam in Mrs. Hauffrey's eyes. "Yes," she said with calm that belied her inner angst.

"Oh my. Well, congratulations, of course."

"Thank you." She turned and strode down the hallway not wanting to give the old windbag any opportunity to ask further questions.

The looks of surprise were all the same. The traffic had never been so high through the downtown veterinarian practice. People wondered in to ask a variety of questions, but their purpose was all the same. To see the pregnant woman.

At first, Toni was amused, but by the afternoon, she was downright pissed. The subtle speculative stares. The overt open mouths. A few didn't even make a pretense of their presence. They walked in, took a look, and stalked out.

Hadn't anyone in this town ever gotten pregnant out of wedlock? Well, there *was* Amanda Jo Haney in high school. But come to think of it, she'd basically been run out of town on a rail. Not that anyone had demanded it. Far from it. Everyone made a pretense of supporting her, but made her life hell behind their hands.

She was stronger than that though. She wasn't a shrinking violet. Shy, yes. Doormat, no. They could all take their sanctimonious BS and stick it where the sun didn't shine.

When four o'clock rolled around she couldn't get out of the office fast enough. Settling behind the wheel of her jeep, she allowed herself a brief moment of melancholy before she cranked the engine and tore out the parking lot like the devil himself was on her tail.

She took the side streets to avoid driving down Main Street. Normally she'd wave to people she knew as she passed, but today her pariah status made her wish she had a paper bag to wear over her head.

When she finally drove into her driveway, she sighed in relief. She walked to the door but saw her elderly neighbors watching her out of the corner of her eye. Turning around, she waved and smiled brightly.

"I ought to sell tickets to this circus," she muttered as she let herself in the house.

She dropped her keys on the table next to her purse and surveyed the empty living room. Only one of the trucks was gone out front, but all three must have gone together, because the house was eerily quiet.

Not looking a gift horse in the mouth, she poured a glass of juice and escaped to the back patio. She sank into one of the lawn chairs and closed her eyes wearily. For someone who spent a great deal of her time practicing obscurity, her newfound bug under a magnifying glass act was giving her a serious stomachache.

It wasn't the fact that everyone thought she'd screwed up. She *had* screwed up. It went way beyond just being a single pregnant woman. She'd acted irresponsibly in a weak moment, and now not only would she have to pay for it, but Simon and their baby would suffer as well.

She had to tell him, but every time she thought of it, her tongue swelled and no words would come out of her mouth. What could she say anyway? *By the way Simon, we had unprotected sex one night when you thought I was your girlfriend and now I'm pregnant.*

A tear slid down her cheek as she berated herself for the hundredth time since that night. She hastily wiped at her face when she heard the sliding door open. Footsteps approached, but she didn't look up.

Simon knelt beside her chair and looked at her in concern. "What's wrong," he asked quietly.

He cupped her cheek and turned her to look back at him. "You've been crying."

He always did have a knack for stating the obvious. She sighed deeply. "Just feeling sorry for myself."

He rose and pulled a chair next to hers. "What's got you down?"

"I'm the new topic of gossip in Cypress. I wore a maternity shirt to work today and Mrs. Hauffrey came in with the poodles."

He winced. "Say no more."

"Yeah."

"Want something to eat? I'm cooking," he said cajolingly.

She gave him a half-hearted smile. "Sure. I'll be there in a minute."

He walked back into the house, and she closed her eyes once more. His handsome face floated teasingly in front of her again. With a shake of her head, she sat up and strode back into the house.

"Hey gorgeous," A.J. sang out, catching her with one arm as she entered the living room. He gave her a quick hug and a kiss on the top of her head.

She grinned despite her sour mood.

"Now that's better," he said approvingly. "You looked like you'd swallowed a lemon when you first walked in."

"Just a watermelon seed," she teased.

He stuck out a hand to her belly. "Hmmm, nope not yet. When's that kid going to pop out anyway?"

"You're in the wrong spot." She moved his hand lower.

"Hey, there it is! It's cute," he said as he massaged the slight swell.

She raised an eyebrow in amusement. "Cute?"

"Quit mauling her, bonehead," Simon said with a scowl. "Dinner's almost done so get your butt over here and set the table."

"What's your hurry, dude?"

"He's got a date," Matt volunteered with a roll of his eyes.

Toni's heart lurched, but she fought to maintain a neutral expression. "Oh? Who's the lucky girl?"

A peculiar expression lit Simon's face. "It's not a date."

"Starla," Matt said in a disgusted voice.

Forgetting neutrality altogether, Toni's mouth dropped open. "Starla? The same Starla who cheated on you just a few months ago?"

"It's not a date," he repeated.

"Are you out of your mind?" she demanded.

Matt's eyes widened in surprise at Toni's raised voice.

"Why on earth would you give her the time of day much less a second chance?" Toni shook her head in disbelief, her face growing hotter.

"I'm not giving her anything," he said defensively. "She just wanted to talk."

She snorted. "Talk my foot. That's fine, Simon. But I won't be around this time to help you pick up the pieces." She whirled around and stomped to her room.

"What was all that about?" Matt murmured.

Simon slowly turned back to the stove. What the heck did she mean help him pick up the pieces? Maybe her pregnancy hormones were raging, or maybe she was upset over the day she'd had.

"She was just saying what you and I are thinking," A.J. said in disgust. "I don't understand why he'd give her the time of day either."

Matt shrugged. "It's his business, I suppose."

Simon turned around. "Thank you, Matt. You are exactly right." He leveled a pointed stare at A.J.

A.J. shrugged. "Sometimes, Simon, you are the biggest fool. If you can't see what's so clearly under your nose you deserve someone like Starla."

He turned and exited the kitchen as well.

"What the hell?" Simon demanded. He looked over at Matt. "Is there something going on I don't know about?"

"Don't ask me," Matt replied. "You know I'm always the last person to know anything around here. But you know, they do have a valid point. Why *are* you going out with Starla?"

"I just want some answers." That and he wanted to get his mind off of Toni. It was getting ridiculous. He was dreaming about her. Fantasizing about her. If he didn't get himself in control soon, he'd do something he'd regret.

What he'd done is pissed her off, though he couldn't quite understand why. But then she'd always been a little overprotective of him and the other guys. Like a mama lion protecting her cubs. Heaven help the girl that ever trod on them.

He grinned. Perhaps he ought to explain to her why he was even speaking to Starla. But then it wouldn't be as fun to see her all riled up. And he couldn't exactly tell her the main reason he was getting out of the house with another woman. He could well envision the shock on her face if he told her about the vivid fantasies he was having about her...naked.

🚌 🚌 🚌

Why was he seeing Starla again? Was he a masochist? Or maybe he wasn't as torn up about her betrayal as he'd let on. It had obviously upset him enough that he indulged in something he never did—drinking.

Toni flopped onto her bed in disgust. Contending with Starla was not a kink she'd planned on having to deal with. It was hard enough just to try and get him to notice her without having to compete with another woman. A woman who had held Simon's heart before.

Her hopes sank a bit further. Starla was everything she wasn't. Beautiful, confident, and most importantly, she wasn't pregnant.

She glanced down at her belly and rubbed absently. If it came down to it, she'd have to confess to Simon. She couldn't allow him to commit to another woman without knowing he had a child.

Chapter Nine

Wednesday and Thursday, Toni stewed about Simon's non-date with Starla. She avoided going to the station even though she normally was a regular visitor during their forty-eight hour shifts. In a way, she didn't want to know anything about his relationship with Starla, but on the other hand, she was going to die if she didn't find out.

Friday morning, she left the house before the guys got home anxious to get the day over with so she could feel Simon out that evening. She fidgeted all day, watching the clock in a sick vigil. She hadn't had an appetite ever since skipping dinner the night of Simon's date.

At three forty-five she was ready to bang her head on the desk in front of her. She tapped her pencil in a steady staccato and watched the seconds tick by.

"Why don't you go on home before you drive me insane," Doc Johnson muttered from behind her.

She whirled around, a guilty flush on her face. "Sorry."

He gave her an indulgent smile. "Go on home. You've been antsy all day. I only have one more animal to see, and Marnie can help me with that one."

Her lips split into a wide grin as she hopped down from the stool. She kissed his wrinkled cheek. "Thanks, doc. I'll see you Monday."

He waved her out the door, and she made a beeline for her jeep. A few minutes later she pulled into her driveway, and to her disappointment saw

Simon's truck was gone. If he was out again with Starla, she was going to hurt someone.

"You're early," A.J. remarked, as she walked into the living room.

"Hello to you, too."

He patted the spot beside him on the couch. "Wanna sit?"

She slid onto the sofa. "Where's Matt and Simon?"

"Simon's running errands, and Matt is getting ready to go over to Stephanie's."

She barely controlled the sigh of relief.

"Something bothering you?"

"No, not at all," she said airily. "Just glad to be home."

She sat in silence for a moment not concentrating on the cop show A.J. was watching. Glancing sideways at him, she said nonchalantly, "So what was the deal with Simon's date with Starla?"

"Ahhh so that's what's bothering you."

She growled under her breath. "No, it's not bothering me. I was merely curious."

"Uh huh. I hear you."

"Well? Do you know anything or not?"

"He was closed mouthed about the whole thing. Didn't stay out late, but wouldn't say a word about what's going on."

She frowned. "What on earth is he thinking?"

A.J. shrugged. "Got me. He must have rocks in his head."

"What am I going to do, A.J.?" she asked softly.

He gave her a sympathetic look. "I don't know, but you better get on the stick."

She leaned her head back and stared up at the ceiling. "I can't compete with her." She turned slightly to look at A.J.

"Please," he said giving her an incredulous look. "She doesn't have anything on you."

"I can think of at least one thing."

"At the risk of pissing you off again, I have to ask, because if I'm right, you've been hung up on Simon for a long time, and yet you got pregnant just a few months ago."

"Yeah, it's twisted, I know," she said bleakly. "Do you think I've ruined my chances?"

"Tell you what," he said suddenly sitting up. "Matt is going over to Steph's in a few minutes, and Simon is due back shortly. I think I'll head out for the evening so the two of you are alone for a few hours. Make the most of it, okay?"

He got up and ruffled her hair as he walked by to his room. At the doorway he paused. "It wouldn't hurt to wear one of those cute little tops. I never knew you had such an impressive bosom." He winked and disappeared through the door.

Toni rolled her eyes and laughed. Why couldn't she have fallen for A.J.? He, at least, found her attractive. Well, if she hoped to make Simon forget all about Starla, she better get up and shower. Right now she smelled like a wet dog.

Foregoing her usual shower, she drew a tub full of water and submerged in the fragrant bubbles of her favorite bath liquid. An hour later, she stepped from the tub, wrapping a towel around her and securing the ends under her arm.

She opted for the white T-shirt and gym shorts, and once again left off the bra. She towel dried her hair, leaving it slightly damp and curling rebelliously. She ventured back into the kitchen, and looked out the window to see Simon's truck in the drive.

The combination of her erratic eating habits over the last two days, and the prolonged warm bath was making her feel lightheaded. She needed to eat something. She rifled through the cabinets, deciding on a can of soup.

Taking out the can opener, she started to remove the top when Simon's voice startled her.

"Hey, Toni."

She whirled around and instantly regretted her actions. The room spun crazily out of control, and she swayed as she attempted to right her equilibrium.

Simon rushed forward, catching her just as her knees buckled. "Toni, what's wrong?" His voice was urgent as he swept her up in his arms and strode to the couch.

"Do you need me to call an ambulance?" he asked as he gently laid her down.

His worried face came into focus as the room stopped spinning.

"No. No, I'm fine," she hastily assured him.

"You don't look fine," he said doubtfully. "Maybe I should take you to the hospital."

"I just need to eat something. I haven't eaten anything today."

"Why not?" he demanded, his face becoming stern. "What the hell are you thinking?"

"I know. It was stupid."

"Don't move," he ordered. "I'll be right back with some soup."

He hurried back to the kitchen, leaving her lying on the couch. A few minutes later he pressed a warm cup in her hands and put an arm around her shoulders to lift her up.

She sipped at the soup, feeling its warmth trail down her throat to her stomach.

"You've got to start taking better care of yourself," he said reproachfully.

He took the cup when she was finished and set it on the coffee table then eased her back onto the couch with the arm that was still supporting her back.

She reached a hand up and placed it on his chest. "Thank you," she whispered.

His face was so close to hers, his lips hovered just out of reach. This was the perfect time. She ached from wanting to feel his lips on hers. Nervously, she moistened her lips and inched closer. His eyes darkened, and was it her imagination, or did he move toward her?

She closed her eyes, preparing to revel in the taste of him when they were both jarred by the telephone ringing. Simon blinked in surprise and shook his head slightly.

The moment was gone. She could see the retreat in his eyes.

Slipping his arm from beneath her, he reached over to pick up the phone off the coffee table.

"Hello?"

She saw a frown cross his face. He looked almost worried. He stood up, seeming to have forgotten her presence on the couch. Turning away, he walked toward his room.

"No, I'm off tomorrow, Starla. I can come by in the morning," she heard as he disappeared down the hall.

What the hell? Anger. Disappointment. There weren't words to accurately portray how she felt at the moment. At least she hadn't kissed him.

With a sigh, she swung her legs over and stood up, testing her legs. They weren't wobbling, thank goodness. And Simon certainly wasn't around to catch her this time.

She picked up the cup she had drank the soup out of and padded into the kitchen. As she rinsed it out in the sink, she heard a tap on the glass of the kitchen door. Looking up, she saw Mike standing outside.

In relief, she hurried over and threw open the door. "Am I glad to see you." In truth, she would have been glad to see anyone. She was ready to crawl into a hole, and she had no desire to face Simon once he finished his tete a tete with Starla.

Mike grinned. "Now that's a nice welcome." He gave her a hug. "How you doing, cutie?"

She glanced back toward Simon's room. "Not so great," she said, expelling a deep breath.

"Uh oh. Did I come at a bad time?"

"Not at all. You're timing is impeccable. Come in for Pete's sake." She gestured him in and shut the door behind him. "What brings you over?"

"I'd rather hear what's bothering you. Anything I can help with?"

"Not unless you're willing to take out a certain brunette with bad timing," she muttered.

He laughed. "She still bugging Simon?"

"Want a beer?" she offered, reaching for the refrigerator handle.

"Sure." He settled onto one of the barstools and leaned his elbows on the bar.

She popped the cap and slid the beer over to him then sat down across from him. "I'm not so sure she's bugging him at all. He doesn't seem to mind her sniffing around."

Mike's face softened. "Damn. Sorry to hear that. But maybe what I came over to ask will help."

She lifted an eyebrow.

"Wanna go to the barbeque with me next weekend? I know you'd probably end up coming with the guys, but it could be a chance to piss Simon off some more." He winked at her as he took a long swig of his beer.

"I don't know," she said doubtfully. "I'm not so sure he gives a flip who I'm going out with."

Mike laughed. "Oh it'll drive him nuts. He already crawled my case at the station."

Her eyes widened. "Wait a minute. You haven't told me about this. What happened?"

She straightened as she heard Simon close his door, and she put a finger to her lips as she heard him walking down the hall.

"Toni, I'm sorry. Are you all right now?" He stopped dead when he took in the two of them sitting at the bar. "Mike? What are you doing here? And Toni, you shouldn't be up." He frowned and continued to walk over. He stopped beside her and laid an arm over her shoulders. Then he glared at Mike.

Mike managed to look amused, his eyes twinkling. "Hey Simon. How's it going?"

Simon ignored him and turned concerned eyes to Toni. "You shouldn't be up. Why don't you go lie back down on the couch, and I'll fix you some more soup."

"What's he babbling about, Toni?" Mike asked with a frown.

Toni fought her annoyance and overwhelming confusion at Simon's peculiar behavior. He'd all but forgotten she existed when Starla called, yet he was practically snarling at Mike. "Oh, nothing. It's no big deal." She fidgeted uncomfortably under the scrutiny of both guys.

"The hell it's not," Simon growled. "You nearly fainted."

"That true, Toni?" Mike asked, concern settling into his eyes.

"It's nothing a little fresh air wouldn't cure. You want to step out on the deck with me?" she asked Mike sweetly.

"Sure," he said, sliding off the barstool. "Let me help you." He walked around and took her elbow to help her up. She nearly laughed aloud at Simon's expression and Mike's blatant exaggeration of her circumstances.

"You should be resting more," he lectured, as they walked toward the door, leaving a scowling Simon behind.

As they closed the sliding doors behind them, Toni giggled. "Okay, you can drop the act now."

"Did you really almost faint?"

"Yeah. No biggie though."

He frowned slightly but didn't pursue it.

"Have a seat," she said gesturing to one of the deck chairs. "Then you can tell me what Simon jumped on you about at the station."

Mike smiled and opted to lean against the deck railing instead. "He doesn't like me seeing you."

She rolled her eyes. "And did he offer an explanation why?"

"Not in so many words. He did threaten to kick my ass though."

She sighed and leaned back beside Mike. "I don't get it, Mike. I thought tonight was the night. I was so close to kissing him. And I think he wanted to kiss me. But then psycho bitch called, and he dropped me like a hot potato."

"Methinks our boy is a bit conflicted," Mike offered.

"Well damn it. I don't want him conflicted. I want him to want me."

"Give it some time," he said soothingly, moving his hand to rub her back. "Let's see what happens this next weekend at the barbeque. If I know Simon, this will all but put the nail in his coffin."

She remained silent. She wished she had Mike's optimism, but she was afraid that the truth of the matter was, Simon had zero interest in her in anything beyond the capacity of a little sister.

"Hey, you wanna go grab something to eat?" he asked suddenly.

She glanced up at him. "I don't know."

"Come on. You need to get out and have a little fun. We could go play some pool afterwards. You used to go down and play with A.J. all the time. You're pregnant, not dead," he reminded her.

"Yes, but if I show up with you, speculation will run rampant you're the father of my baby," she said lightly.

"I should be so lucky," he said with a wink. "Now come on. Let's get out of here and leave Simon to go nuts wondering what we're doing."

Chapter Ten

Simon was waiting when A.J. walked through the door. He picked up his keys off the bar and shoved his wallet in his pocket. "Come on, A.J.. We're going to go play pool."

"We are?" A.J. asked, a startled look on his face.

"Yeah, come on. I'll drive."

A.J. followed behind as they walked out to Simon's truck. "May I ask why we're going to play pool?"

Simon slid into the seat and started the engine. He looked over at A.J. "Because Toni and Mike are going to be there, and I want to make damn sure he doesn't do something stupid." He was still pissed off at Toni for going off after she'd had such a close call. And why Mike would take her out to a freaking bar after he knew she had nearly fainted, he couldn't fathom, but it further solidified his opinion that Mike was in no way suitable to take Toni out.

"Oh no, not this again," A.J. said opening his door again. "I've already sacrificed a date with the put out queen to spy on them once. You can count me out this time."

"A.J., get your ass back in the truck," Simon said impatiently.

A.J. paused with one leg out the door. "Why are we doing this, Simon? Clearly, Toni sees something in the guy she likes. What if he's the father of her baby? Have you ever thought about that?"

Rage boiled through him at the thought of Mike getting Toni pregnant. He gripped the steering wheel until his fingers ached. No, Mike couldn't be the guy. It didn't make sense. He hadn't ever called Toni until well after she found out she was pregnant.

"Dude, cool it. It was just a thought."

"It was a dumb thought," he snapped. "Toni nearly fainted tonight. She hasn't been eating right, and the last thing she needs is to be hanging out in a bar with Mike Sanders."

A.J. slid back into the seat. "Whoa, she did what?"

Simon threw the truck in reverse and roared backwards out of the drive. "She almost dropped on the kitchen floor. She said she hadn't eaten much, and she seemed pretty shaky. Then Mike shows up and suddenly they're going out to play pool. The jerk even knew she wasn't well because I told him."

A.J. frowned. "But if Toni wanted to go…"

Simon cut him off with a snort. "I don't know what her deal is lately. She's not herself at all."

"I see, and you're saving her from herself?"

"I don't know what I'm doing," he muttered, wishing he had some sort of clue.

"Well at least you admit it," A.J. said dryly. "So what exactly are we going to do?

"Play pool, what else?"

"Of course. What was I thinking? We're not doing anything remotely resembling spying or interfering. Just a harmless game of pool. Which you happen to have not played, oh in at least two years."

"Shut up."

Ten minutes later, they pulled up to Benny's the local bar and all around hang out place, and Simon parked by Mike's truck. The haunt was a favorite with the fire and EMS crew. He noted several familiar vehicles. But it was no place for a pregnant woman. The smoke alone would likely send her into premature labor.

"Dude, if you walk in there wearing that scowl, you're going to clear the place. Chill out."

He scowled at A.J., but he relaxed his expression as they stepped inside the dimly lit interior. He scanned the array of people gathered, some sitting at the bar, a few couples dancing as the jukebox blared the latest country song by Toby Keith.

As he and A.J. walked toward the back where the three pool tables were, several hellos rang out. He recognized several faces from work and the ambulance service. He nodded but didn't stop. His focus now on the farthest table.

Toni stood beside Mike, his arm casually over her shoulders as they waited for the guy across the table to take his shot. Anger surged through him. He started to stalk across the room and tear Mike's arm out of his socket, but he reigned himself in. What the hell was wrong with him?

A.J. had a stupid smug grin on his face, and Simon had the urge to smash his teeth in. Shaking his head in an effort to clear his murderous thoughts, Simon leaned over the end of the bar and motioned for a beer.

"So," A.J. drawled. "What now?"

Toni's tinkling laughter filtered across the noise of the room, and Simon's gaze jerked back to where she stood. She was looking up at Mike, apparently laughing at something he had said. She looked radiant. No, she looked damn beautiful.

Mike reached over and tucked a curl behind her ear, and Simon slammed his beer back on the bar. "That's it." He surged forward, A.J. chuckling behind him.

"I wouldn't miss this for the world."

"Shut the hell up, A.J. Toni's your friend too. Start acting like you give a damn."

A.J. caught his arm and swung him around, his eyes blazing. "If you care for her so much, you'd pull your head out of your ass and get a clue."

"What the hell are you talking about?" Had the entire world gone crazy? Toni hanging out with Mike. A.J. acting like he had a bug up his ass. Matt was the only normal one left, and he existed in his own little world anyway.

Before A.J. could continue, he heard Toni's voice call out. "Simon? A.J.? What are you guys doing here?"

"You're in for it now," A.J. said in a low voice.

"Toni?" He actually managed to inflect genuine surprise in his voice as he walked toward the pool table. "What on earth are you doing here?"

She frowned slightly, but damn, she still looked beautiful. The slight bulge of her stomach barely peeked out of the swirls of her shirt. The material gathered tightly around her breasts, emphasizing the gentle swell at the neckline.

"The question is what are you doing here? I didn't realize you came in here much."

"I don't. Well I do, but not all the time," he amended quickly.

"I haven't seen you in here for at least a year," Mike said casually.

He glared at Mike then glanced back at Toni, irritated that Mike had slipped an arm around her waist.

"You shouldn't be here, Toni. If Mike had any sense, he'd have you home in bed."

"Now there's a thought," Mike said with barely disguised amusement.

"Over my dead body," Simon growled. "Toni's not your next one night stand."

Toni stepped forward, anger sparking in her soft brown eyes. "I think that's enough, Simon. What Mike and I do or don't do is none of your business."

He flinched. It was the truth, and he was making a royal ass of himself. But damn it, what on earth had gotten into Toni? First she got pregnant and was as tightlipped as a clam about the father and then she started making rounds with the bed hoppingest guy in Cypress.

"You're right. It is none of my business. But I'm concerned about you, Toni. If you won't take care of yourself, someone has to."

She flushed a dull red. Embarrassment clouded her eyes, and he immediately regretted his outburst. The last thing he wanted to do was hurt her. "You weren't so concerned once your little girlfriend called," she snapped.

"Starla? What the hell does she have to do with this?"

Her lips compressed in a thin line. Then she looked up at Mike. "Can you take me home?" Her soft voice wavered, and Simon mentally kicked himself again.

"You okay?" Mike asked in a low voice, but Simon heard him clearly. He didn't like the inference that he had upset her. But even A.J. was looking at him in disgust.

"Toni," Simon began, but she was no longer looking at him. Mike shouldered by him, his hand at the small of Toni's back.

"Nice going, Andrews," Mike muttered.

Simon closed his eyes and clenched his fists beside him. What the hell was happening to him? He was turning into a first class turd.

"Well. That was a success," A.J. said as Toni and Mike left the pool hall.

"Cut the sarcasm, A.J. I know I was an ass."

"That you were. If you're done making an ass of yourself, can we go home now?"

"Yeah, whatever." He stalked toward the door, feeling like a complete moron. He'd rather spend the next twelve hours fighting a damn fire than go home and face an upset Toni.

🚌 🚌 🚌

"So, I'll see you Saturday?" Mike asked as Toni slid from his truck.

She attempted a smile though her mind was whirling. "Yeah. And thanks for tonight. I really did have fun."

"No problem. I think your boy is contemplating the funny farm at the moment."

She frowned. "I have no idea what to make of him right now. He forgot about me quick enough when Starla called. Then he follows us to Benny's and acts like I'm an irresponsible teenager."

He grinned. "It'll probably get a lot worse before he wakes up and smells the coffee."

"I wish I had your confidence, Mike. I'll see you later, okay?" She shut the door and waved as he pulled away then she hurried inside.

She set her purse down on the bar and stood a moment not sure what to do next. Simon had acted weird. The whole evening had been a venture into the twilight zone. Had she really contemplated kissing Simon just a few hours ago?

In hindsight she was glad Starla had called. She wasn't at all sure her seduction plan was working, and at any rate, it was too soon to kiss him. She didn't want him to kiss her because he was worried about her. She wanted him to do it because he couldn't help himself.

She turned when she heard Simon's truck pull up. For a fleeting moment, she wanted to retreat to her room, but she wasn't that much of a coward. Besides, he'd been a complete jerk, and she wasn't going to let him off the hook that easily.

She leaned against the counter and waited for them to come in. A.J. was first. He gave her an apologetic look, but remained silent as Simon tramped in behind him.

He had the grace to look exceedingly guilty as he caught her gaze. He glanced over at A.J. "You mind if I talk to Toni alone?"

"Ah damn. You mean I don't get to see you grovel?" At Simon's glare, he threw up his hands. "Okay, okay, I'm going."

As A.J. retreated to his room, Simon turned to look at her once more. "Toni, I'm sorry. Really I am. I was just worried about you. You didn't see how pale you were when you almost fainted. I just didn't think you should be going out, and I was pissed that Mike didn't take better care with you."

His explanation came out in a rush. She pushed off the edge of the counter and moved closer to him. "I appreciate your concern, Simon. Truly, I do. But you embarrassed me." A hot flush swept over her face all over again as she remembered the stares of the entire crowd at Benny's on her.

Regret sparked in his eyes. "I'm a jerk, Toni. I swear I don't know what came over me. My only excuse is I do *not* trust Mike as far as I could throw him. He'll use you and be on to his next woman in a week."

Another flush stole over her face. "I'm glad you think me that desirable."

"Damn it, Toni. That's not what I meant. You're beautiful. One of the most beautiful girls I've ever known. But Mike only wants one thing when it comes to women."

"Well at least I wouldn't have to worry about getting pregnant," she said ruefully.

It was the wrong thing to say. She knew it as soon as she let it slip. Fury rose in his eyes, and he closed the distance between them. "Tell me you aren't sleeping with him, Toni."

Her mouth fell open. "I'm not telling you anything. Who I sleep with is none of your business."

"You're not that kind of girl, Toni," he began.

She arched an eyebrow, her anger building by the minute. And her humiliation. "What kind of girl is that?" she asked softly. "Because I go out on a date, I'm suddenly relegated to the town slut? Or is it because I'm pregnant?" She stared pointedly at him.

He gripped her shoulders and gave her a slight shake. "Don't put words in my mouth. I have never thought less of you because you're pregnant. I just don't want to see you hurt. I care a lot about you, Toni. And I'll kill anyone who dares call you a slut."

She couldn't summon a response, nor could she retain her anger. Her shoulders sagged. "I'm not mad, Simon. Just embarrassed. I appreciate your worrying over me, but I wish you'd lay off Mike. He's not such a bad guy. In fact, he's been a pretty great friend."

Simon frowned again. "You have plenty of friends. You don't need him."

Toni laughed. "If I didn't know better, I'd say you were jealous."

She could have kicked herself. He stared strangely at her as if she'd grown another head or something.

"Your color is better," he said out of the blue.

She blinked at the rapid change in conversation.

He reached out to smooth her hair off her cheek. "I'm sorry I embarrassed you, sweetheart. I was an ass. I won't lie and say it doesn't set my teeth on edge to see you going out with Mike, but I promise to try and accept it for your sake."

She smiled at his concession. If he only knew why she was going out with Mike. Would he be relieved or pissed?

"Now, can I persuade you to go to bed and get some rest?" he asked.

"You won't have to twist my arm too hard," she said with a smile. "But I'm only going because I'm tired." She started to walk past him.

To her surprise, he caught her by the waist and enfolded her in his arms. He buried his face in her hair, his words muffled. "I don't like you mad at me."

She drew away and stared up at him. She let loose a mental groan. His lips hovered temptingly above hers. She pushed away from him before she did something stupid. Like kiss him.

Chapter Eleven

The next morning Toni slept in—the extra hours of sleep much needed. She showered and dressed then ventured into the kitchen to scrounge up breakfast.

"Morning, guys," she called out as she saw Matt and A.J. seated at the bar shoveling down a bowl of cereal.

The both looked up and mumbled a greeting.

She poured a glass of juice and sat down across from them. "What's on the agenda for today?"

They both gave her blank stares and she laughed. "I'll take that as a big fat nothing."

Matt shrugged. "Simon left early. Have no idea where he went. I don't really have any plans to speak of."

Toni frowned. She knew where Simon was. The juice tasted sour on her tongue and she put it down. "You not seeing Stephanie today?"

He gave her an uneasy glance and shrugged again. "Probably not."

A.J. lifted a brow and put down his spoon. "Trouble in paradise?" He raised the bowl to his lips and noisily chugged the remaining milk then set the bowl back down with a bang.

Toni laughed. "You're such a barbarian, A.J."

He gave her a wounded look.

Matt ignored A.J.'s question and the joking between Toni and A.J.

Toni and A.J. exchanged curious glances. "I'm hitting the shower," A.J. said, and Toni knew he was leaving so she and Matt could be alone.

"So what's up with you and Stephanie?" she asked when A.J. ambled off.

"Uh, nothing major. Just taking some time to think about things," he said vaguely.

"I thought maybe she was the one. You guys seemed perfect for each other."

Matt shifted uncomfortably on the barstool and glanced away for a moment. "Well, the thing is, I think she might be the one too."

Toni leaned forward, excitement building within her. "But, Matt, that's great!"

He leveled a hard stare at her. "Think about it, Toni. If I asked her to marry me, everything would change. *Everything*."

She didn't try and hide her confusion. "I don't understand."

He sighed and shoved his cereal bowl away from him. "The thing is, I've been thinking hard about asking her to marry me. I really love her," he added softly.

"So what's the but?"

"But...there's the little issue of living arrangements. Either Stephanie and I buy a house, which neither of us can afford right now, or we make Simon and A.J. find another place to live so we can live here."

"And I would still be a third wheel," she said, comprehension dawning.

"No," he said emphatically. "This is your house and there is no way I'd have you move out. Especially not with you pregnant."

"I really screwed up didn't I," she whispered. "And not just for me. But I'm screwing it up for you too."

"Damn it, Toni. This is why I didn't want to say anything." He reached across the bar and grasped her hand. "Look at me."

She stared back at him, the utter seriousness reflected in his brown eyes.

"There are a lot of factors involved here. One, you need me. And," he said effectively cutting off her forthcoming protest, "I like the setup we have here. I'm not sure I'm ready to give that up."

Toni thought back to the conversation she'd had with Simon in the park. Much of their talk had surrounded the same thing Matt has just said. No one wanted to give up the current situation.

And if she were honest, she knew she had no desire to see her brother married and moved off or the four of them separated and no longer roommates. But things had to change. They always did. And nothing lasts forever.

She sounded like a whole book of trite clichés.

She cleared her throat. "I don't know what to say, Matt. But sooner or later things will change. You guys will eventually want to settle down, and that means we won't always live together. But that doesn't mean we can't still hang out together. Get together on the weekends."

"I know all of that," Matt said. "I just can't fathom being the one to mess up everything. It would be different if Simon had married Starla or A.J. decided to get married, God forbid."

Toni laughed at the image of A.J. getting married.

"I always imagined being the last one to get hitched. I figured you'd get married and move out and then the other guys would move out and when I got married, we'd live here. But I can't push everyone out, and I'm damn sure not leaving you when you need me the most."

Tears gathered in Toni's eyes, and she hastily brushed them away. It had never occurred to her how dedicated everyone was to keeping the arrangement that had suited them for years. The idea of change was abhorrent to them all, and each one was fighting against the idea. She'd done her share of cringing at the thought.

But for the first time, she allowed herself to think of just how affected they would be by her pregnancy. And aside from the fact Simon had to be told about his impending fatherhood, the situation was impossible. If she stayed, they would all feel a responsibility to both her and her baby.

She knew them well enough to know they would shove aside their own wants if they thought she needed them. She would do the same for them. It's just the way it had always been. But it didn't have to be.

And how would it affect the baby if after living with three father figures, one or all of them married and moved away? It could be potentially devastating. It would be far better if she moved and released them from any obligation they felt for her.

She'd let them talk her out of moving in the beginning, but even then, she knew it had been the best idea. She'd allowed her sadness over the idea of losing them to sway her when it would have been in their best interest if she had moved. Would Simon be back with Starla even now if he weren't worried about her?

The thought sickened her. As much as she loved him, she did not want to be seen as a hindrance to his happiness. And now Matt was ready to settle down and get married, but his concern for her kept him from moving forward.

"I don't like your expression," Matt said with a frown. "I wish I hadn't said anything."

"I'm glad you did," she said softly. "You've given me a lot to think about. A veritable wake up call."

His frown deepened.

"I think it would be best if I did go ahead and move out."

Matt surged up from his seat, his eyes blazing. "Damn it, Toni. That is not why I brought the subject up. There is no way, *no way*, I'm going to let you move out right now. And certainly not because you think I would benefit. This is your house. Your *home*. It's where you grew up. You and your child deserve a home, not a shoddy apartment or trailer somewhere."

"Sit down, Matt," she said gently.

He stared at her for a long moment then slowly sank back onto the stool.

"Think about it for a minute. As long as I'm living here with you guys you're all going to put off your own wants and needs because you think I'm still a little girl you have to protect and take care of."

"But—"

"Let me finish," she said putting her hand out. "It will only get worse when the baby is born. I don't want any of you to sacrifice your happiness for me. I can't stand the thought of it. For everyone's sake, including mine, I need to find a place for me and the baby to live. Then we'll all feel free to make decisions regarding our futures without worry."

He shook his head adamantly. "What if something happened to you while you were pregnant?"

"It's not like I wouldn't have a phone," she said dryly.

"I don't want you to move," he said simply.

"I think it might just be time to step out from under yours and Simon's and A.J.'s protective arms. I've stayed because I've been comfortable, but I've never given thought to the sacrifices you've made for me."

"It's been no sacrifice," he said fiercely. "You've taken care of us far more than we've ever taken care of you."

She chuckled. "That might just be true, but maybe it's time for that to change. I have a baby to take care of now." Her mind began to work again. There had to be a solution. "What if I stayed until the baby is born and then moved? It would give everyone the time to get used to the idea, and it would give me the time to save up some money."

"But is that what you want?" he asked, studying her intently. "Because if you're doing it because you think it would be best for us, forget it. You and the baby are more important right now."

"I won't lie and say I won't miss you all terribly. But I'll visit. Okay, I'll visit a lot." She grinned slightly. "And hopefully you guys will visit me." And maybe, just maybe, if things went the way they were supposed to, Matt and Stephanie wouldn't be the only ones to get together.

But she couldn't think of her and Simon right now. Matt obviously wanted to make a commitment to Stephanie, and she didn't want to keep her brother from his happiness.

"If you move, I'll buy out your half of the house," he said.

She shook her head. "Consider it my wedding gift to you and Stephanie."

He shook his head just as adamantly.

"We'll talk about it when the time comes," she said in exasperation.

"What will we talk about?" A.J. said as he sauntered back up to the bar.

"That I'm going to move out after the baby's born," she said lightly. There was no reason to keep it a secret. The sooner everyone knew, the faster it would be dealt with. She steeled herself for his protest, but then A.J. was the most easygoing of the bunch.

He merely looked at her. "Are you sure that's what you want?"

She nodded then turned back to Matt. "So, now that we got that out of the way, when do you plan to pop the question?"

A.J.'s mouth fell open. "Seriously? You're asking Stephanie to marry you?"

"I'm thinking about it," Matt corrected.

"Hey man, that's great. She's a wonderful girl." He slapped Matt on the back, a broad grin on his face.

"Thanks. I think so too."

The doorknob rattled and Simon walked in the door, dumping his keys on the bar. He looked curiously between the three standing at the bar. Toni tensed, the jubilation she felt for Matt fading.

"Did I miss something? You three look like you're celebrating."

"Matt's getting hitched," A.J. said with a grin.

"Might be getting hitched," Matt said, elbowing A.J. in the gut.

"Really? That's great. When's the big day?"

Toni watched as the world around her began to change. No, it had been changing for a while. Ever since the fateful night she'd had sex with Simon. And there wasn't a damn thing she could do to reverse the consequences.

She tuned out the guys who were in an animated conversation as to how best for Matt to propose to Stephanie. Somehow, she'd always imagine she would be the first to get married and move out. At this rate, she'd be the last.

"I guess we'll all be looking for a new place to live and not just Toni," A.J. spoke up, yanking her from her thoughts.

Simon frowned. "What? I thought we agreed she was staying here."

"Somehow I don't see Matt and Stephanie wanting two guys, a sister-in-law and a baby crowding in on their marriage," she pointed out. "Matt and I have discussed it, and I'll move out after the baby's born."

Simon looked thunderstruck. "There's no reason the three of us couldn't find a place."

A.J. leaned back and remained silent. In fact, everyone shut up. "And what about when you and A.J. decide to get married? That means me and the tikester will be moving again. No, I'd rather find a permanent place and make a home for me and my child," she said firmly.

Simon opened his mouth to speak then shut it again.

Matt ran a hand through his hair. "You see, Toni? This is precisely why I didn't want to get into this yet. What we have here works. We're a family."

Simon nodded. Even A.J. acknowledged it by a slight inclination of his head.

"Even families have to grow up and move on," she insisted. "And I can't imagine Simon or A.J. either one wanting you to sacrifice your happiness just to keep us all together."

At that, both Simon and A.J. shook their heads.

She walked around the bar to where Matt sat and wrapped her arms tightly around him. "I love you," she said fiercely. "And I want you to be happy. Sure it will suck for a while. Do you remember when I left for college?"

Matt chuckled close to her ear.

"We'll get over it, and we'll still be a family. Only now, Stephanie will be a part of it."

He returned her hug, nearly squeezing the breath from her. "I love you too, little sister."

She drew away then glanced back at Simon and A.J. "There is one catch, you know. You'll have to have us all over on Sundays to watch football. Stephanie will just have to understand if she's going to marry you." She winked broadly at Matt, and his face relaxed into a huge smile.

As she looked around the kitchen, the only one not smiling was Simon.

Chapter Twelve

He'd been unable to shake his irritation ever since Toni had informed them all she was moving out and Matt had announced he was proposing to Stephanie. He felt betrayed.

Simon sat at the kitchen bar waiting for the others to get ready for the annual fire and rescue barbeque held at the firehouse. He had almost no enthusiasm to go, but neither did he want to stay at home and stew.

For the last several years, he'd lived with people he considered his family. His best friends. And now in the space of a few months things were going to change forever. It was thoroughly depressing. Almost as depressing as Toni dating Mike Sanders.

As if conjuring him up by his thoughts, he looked up to see Mike knocking on the kitchen door. With a scowl, he motioned him in. "What the hell are you doing over here? Aren't you supposed to be working?" Simon asked.

"Yeah, I just ran over to pick Toni up for the barbeque."

Irritation surged over Simon. "You left work to pick her up when we're all heading over there anyway? She could have ridden with us."

Mike shrugged. "Slow morning and you're only five minutes away. Besides, I asked Toni to go with me."

Remembering how angry he had made Toni last time, Simon bit his tongue and turned away. "She'll be out in a minute."

"Mike, what you doing here?" A.J. asked as he walked into the kitchen.

"Picking Toni up."

A.J. frowned. "She could've ridden with us."

Mike rolled his eyes. "Can you just get her? I have to get back to the station pretty quick."

"Toni," A.J. hollered toward her room. "Loverboy's here to get you."

"Don't be an ass," Mike said with a scowl.

Toni appeared seconds later, and Simon did an instant double take. In a word, she looked fantastic. She glowed from head to toe. And her shirt. He had the insane urge to throw a jacket over her to cover the neckline. Was it all due to pregnancy or had she always looked so damn beautiful?

"Hi, Mike, you ready to go?" she asked with a smile in his direction.

Jealousy slammed hard into Simon's chest leaving him nearly shaking. Jealousy. Good God. He was losing his ever-loving mind.

"I'll see you guys in a bit?" she asked turning to look at him and A.J.

"Yeah, we're coming now," Simon said, picking up his keys.

Mike led Toni out with a hand to her back, and Simon followed behind seething the entire way. And as usual, A.J. was wearing his smug little grin.

🚒 🚒 🚒

"This isn't working," Toni said, as she and Mike pulled up to the firehouse.

A multitude of cars and trucks were parked at the station, and in the vacant lot adjoining the building, a large barbeque grill had been set up. Firemen, ambulance personal and even some of the sheriff's department were gathered, laughing and joking over cold beer.

Mike turned the engine off and slid around in his seat to face her. "What's not working?"

"This whole charade," she said with a sigh. "I feel pretty stupid about it now. I don't want to drive a wedge between me and Simon, and I think that's precisely what I'm doing. If I can't have him in the way I wanted, I at least want to continue our friendship."

"That's understandable." His eyes softened in sympathy. "I'm sorry, Toni. I wish I could help."

"You have helped." She reached over and squeezed his hand. "You've been a great friend."

"So does this mean you're dumping me?" he asked, adopting a mock wounded look.

She laughed. "I doubt anyone's ever dumped you."

Simon and A.J. pulled up beside them, and Toni turned to get out of the truck. She could feel Simon boring holes in her back as she followed Mike into the station house.

As they walked in, Matt called out a greeting. He and Stephanie were talking with the fire chief and his wife. Toni smiled and waved, feeling a quick moment of happiness that Matt had found the woman he wanted to marry.

Within moments of their arrival, a game of flag football formed and Toni was cajoled into playing. The fire crew was pitted against rescue, and Toni was recruited by ambulance since she had worked dispatch in the past.

Amidst cries of traitor, she joined her teammates against Matt, Mike, A.J. and the other members of their fire squad. Curiously, Simon stood back, a drink in hand, broodingly silent. Toni frowned as she lined up across from A.J. "What eating him?" she asked nodding in Simon's direction.

A.J. shrugged. "Dunno. He's been like that all morning."

She glanced back over again as the football was snapped and froze. A.J. shot by her but her gaze was riveted to the woman standing beside Simon. What the hell was she doing here?

"You're way too easy," A.J. teased as he brushed back by her to line up.

She blinked then flushed. She'd missed the entire play. "What's she doing here?" she hissed as she tried to divert her attention to the game.

A.J. glanced over his shoulder. "Talking to Simon it looks like."

"My, aren't you the observant one," she said sourly.

He chuckled. "C'mon, let's play. You can get out all that pent up aggression."

"Just remember you asked for it," she muttered as she drove her shoulder into his stomach.

Thirty minutes later, the score was tied and the barbeque was almost ready. But rescue had the ball and they weren't conceding defeat just to go eat. They formed the huddle and Steve, a paramedic Toni had gone to school with, gestured at her. "Give the ball to her. No one will mess with a pregnant woman."

She laughed. "Don't be so sure about that. A.J. is out for revenge after I laid him out awhile ago."

"You up for it, Toni?" Rick asked. "I'll hand it off and run interference for you down the field."

"Oh sure, make the pregnant woman run," she grumbled, but grinned good-naturedly.

They lined up and she grinned evilly at A.J. "Don't get in my way, pretty boy."

The play started and after a fake pass, Rick tossed the ball to Toni then shoved A.J. out of the way. She tucked the ball under her arm and took off down the field toward the appointed goal line.

Laughter rose as Fire figured out they'd been had. But Mike wasn't so easy a sale. He cut her off before she could reach the goal line and scooped her up ball and all. "Interception!" he yelled as he took off toward the opposite end of the field.

She shouted with laughter. "Put me down, you lug!" She bounced on his shoulder, the ground spinning below her as he wrapped an arm around her legs and increased his speed.

And just as suddenly as she had been plucked from the ground, suddenly she was flat on her back, Mike sprawled on top of her. She sucked in air, or tried to as she wheezed for breath.

"Oh crap, Toni, are you all right?" Mike demanded as he scrambled up.

"What happened?" she croaked.

"The moron fell on you," A.J. offered as he appeared beside her. Concern filled his eyes as he bent down. "Are you okay?"

And then Simon was over her, shoving Mike and A.J. back. "Don't move," he instructed.

"I'm okay," she protested. "Just got the wind knocked out of me. Don't go all paramedic on me, Simon. There's enough of those around."

The crowd gathered around her laughed in relief. But Simon was still frowning. He glared up at Mike. "That was a dumbass thing to do, Sanders.

You don't sling a pregnant woman over your shoulder and go barging down the field."

Mike remained silent to Toni's relief. She had no desire to be the center of an argument. "I'm fine, Simon," she said firmly. "Now help me up."

Strong hands lifted her to a standing position and remained on her shoulders as she stood a moment collecting herself. She caught Matt's concerned gaze across the field and nodded reassuringly at him.

"Guess the game's over," Rick announced.

"The food's ready anyway," Steve remarked, sliding his arm around his wife, Tracy.

"Are you okay, Toni?" Tracy asked, placing a hand on Toni's shoulder.

She smiled at the other woman. "I'm fine, Tracy. Thanks though.

"You know these men," Tracy said, rolling her eyes. "All brawn and absolutely no brain."

"Hey, I resemble that remark," Mike protested. He slid an arm around Toni's waist, apology reflected in his eyes. "I'm sorry, Toni. Simon's right. It was stupid and I could have hurt you."

"At least he admits it," Simon muttered.

"Enough already," she said. "I'm ready to eat."

The crowd filtered out, all heading to the two tables that had been set up by the barbeque pit. Simon lagged behind as Toni slowly walked toward the others. "Are you sure you're not hurt?" he persisted.

"Simon, I'm fine," she said in exasperation.

He put an arm around her shoulders and walked back with her. As they approached the others, Toni could feel Starla staring at them. There was no malevolence in her eyes, just thoughtful reflection.

Toni felt a pang of guilt. What if Simon really wanted to be with Starla? What if she was the only one who could make him happy? She shook her head, then disguised the gesture by smoothing her hair with her hand. No. She couldn't countenance Starla being the right woman for Simon after she had betrayed him by sleeping with another man.

The line had formed as the barbeque ribs and chicken were laid out on the table. Delicious smells filled the air and several groaned their appreciation.

Every year the barbeque was eagerly awaited as it was generally accepted Chief Maxwell cooked the best darn barbeque in southeast Texas.

The talk centered around the latest fire or ambulance calls. The sheriff's deputies added their stories of the latest weirdos they had arrested. Then, of course, the conversation settled on something they all appreciated. Football.

Toni sat to the side to eat, watching the others. A.J. was flirting with Darcy, an EMT with the ambulance service. She grinned. He was barking up the wrong tree with that one. Darcy knew far too much about A.J. to ever give him the time of day, and if A.J. knew just how marriage minded Darcy was, he'd drop her like a bad habit.

Her attention turned to Matt and Stephanie, and once again she felt a pang at their obvious devotion to one another. Stephanie was a sweet girl and perfect for Matt. Toni just hoped Stephanie felt as much for Matt as he did her.

Then her gaze slid to Starla who stood several feet away from where Simon was conversing with Chief Maxwell. It escaped Toni why Starla had even shown up, but then the barbeque always got its fair share of people who invited themselves. Before the day was over, most of the town would probably end up coming by.

A series of shrill beeps split the air and a chorus of groans soon followed. The on duty guys, including Mike, scrambled up and headed for the inside of the station. He stopped on his way by and offered an apology. "I'm sorry, Toni. If I'm not back by the time you get ready to leave, can you get a ride home with Simon and A.J.?"

She nodded and he hurried off. A few minutes later, the fire truck left the station and the party resumed. She picked at the rest of her food, her appetite practically non-existent.

A curious tightening in her abdomen had her shifting in her seat to alleviate the discomfort. After a few minutes, she got up and threw her plate away in the garbage. She stood watching everyone else, fidgeting from one foot to another. She couldn't explain the slight unease she felt.

In relief, she turned her attention to Matt, who stood and motioned for silence. Stephanie stood beside him, smiling shyly at the people now staring at her and Matt. Toni's chest tightened and a smile found its way to her mouth. She knew what was coming.

"I have good news, folks," Matt announced, a broad grin on his face. He glanced down at Stephanie and squeezed her hand. "Stephanie has agreed to marry me."

The people gathered erupted in cheers and whistles and Matt and Stephanie were immediately swarmed as everyone came to offer congratulations, hugs and handshakes.

Toni stood back, her smile growing ever wider. It was wonderful to see Matt so happy. He found her gaze and she smiled even bigger. He returned her smile then mouthed I love you.

She blew him a kiss then wiped quickly at her eyes. When the crowd around them lessened, Toni walked over and enfolded Matt in her biggest hug. "I'm happy for you," she whispered.

He gripped her harder.

Then she drew away and smiled at Stephanie. "Congratulations, Steph." She hugged her future sister-in-law.

"Thank you, Toni. Are you sure you're okay with this?" she asked anxiously, holding on to both of Toni's hands as they drew apart.

"You're kidding right?" she asked in mock surprise. "Anyone who can make him smile that big has my blessing." She winked at Stephanie. "You two make a great couple."

Stephanie relaxed and settled back into Matt's side.

"Do you have a date yet?" Toni asked.

Stephanie looked up at Matt. "We thought next summer."

Matt nodded his agreement.

Once again, Toni felt the discomfort of guilt. She had a feeling if it weren't for the fact she was pregnant, they would marry much earlier. But as it was, they wouldn't have a house to live in until she and the other guys moved out.

She turned away and excused herself then headed inside the station to go to the bathroom. A few minutes alone would do wonders before her smile cracked in front of everyone else. And she did have to pee awfully bad.

But when she pulled down her underwear and sat down on the toilet, she forgot all about everything but the faint smudges of blood in her panties.

Her stomach clenched and panic swelled in her throat. She closed her eyes and tried to remember the passage in her pregnancy book about blood. Damn it, there were only forty different reasons a pregnant woman could spot, but the one uppermost in her mind was miscarriage.

Chapter Thirteen

Toni walked outside, her eyes seeking A.J. When she zeroed in on his location, she made a beeline for him. Thankfully, he was on the edge of the crowd of people so they wouldn't attract any attention.

She walked up to him and touched him on the arm. He stopped talking to the sheriff's deputy and turned to her. Alarm flashed in his eyes. Was her fear that obvious?

Before he could voice any concern, she tightened her grip on his arm. "Can I speak to you a minute?" she asked in a low voice, hoping not to be overheard by anyone else.

He followed her over a few feet then immediately demanded to know what was wrong. She swallowed the rising panic and tried to speak calmly so as not to alarm him further. "Can you take me home?"

He frowned. "Sure, but what's wrong?"

"I'm spotting," she whispered.

His eyes widened. "Let me get Simon and Matt. We need to get you to the hospital."

She caught his arm as he turned. "No."

"Why not?" he demanded.

"Shhh," she hissed. "I don't want to make a big scene. I don't want to ruin Matt and Stephanie's moment, and Simon is busy talking to Starla. Can you just take me home? Simon can get a ride with either Starla or Matt."

"I'm taking you to the hospital," he said stubbornly.

She gritted her teeth. "First I want to go home so I can call my OB. It may be nothing. I've read that spotting is common with pregnant women. I just want to be safe."

"Then come on," he said, taking her arm and leading her toward the truck.

They climbed into the truck and A.J. backed up and roared off. "I don't like this," he said. "I should be taking you to the hospital."

"And maybe you will. I just want to see what my doctor has to say. I just didn't want to make a big to do in front of everyone back there."

"Was it the fall?" he demanded.

"I don't know," she said honestly. "I don't know anything at all."

As if sensing how close she was to losing what semblance of control she had, he reached across and squeezed her hand tightly. "It'll be okay, Toni." But she could hear the uncertainty in his voice.

When they got home, A.J. ushered her in. "Sit down on the couch. I'll bring you the phone."

She sat down in the corner of the couch and curled her feet underneath her. Her hand smoothed over her stomach, feeling the bulge. Tears stung her eyelids, and she blinked rapidly to keep them at bay. She couldn't lose her baby. She'd never even told Simon it was his.

A.J. sat down beside her and handed her the phone. He placed his hand on her back and rubbed up and down in an effort to comfort her as she punched in the number for her doctor.

After leaving a message with his answering service, she hung up and looked helplessly over at A.J. "I can't lose this baby, A.J."

"I know, sweetheart," he said enfolding her in his arms. He rocked her back and forth rubbing up and down her back. "Are you sure you don't want me to just take you in to the ER and get you checked out?"

She shook her head. "I'll see what the doctor says first."

The sound of the kitchen door opening had Toni wiping her eyes frantically. She looked over to see Simon standing by the bar staring at her and A.J.

"What the hell is going on?" he demanded. "Toni, why are you crying?"

Simon took in Toni's tear-stained face and fear seized him. What was wrong? Why had she and A.J. left the barbeque? The phone ringing interrupted his question, and Toni quickly snatched up the receiver.

A.J. stood up and walked over as Toni murmured in low tones to whoever it was on the phone. He strained to hear, but A.J. spoke up in a whisper. "She started spotting."

Simon caught his breath. "Why didn't you take her to the hospital?"

"I tried," A.J. said shaking his head. "She wanted to come here and call her doc first."

Simon ran a hand through his hair and blew out his breath in irritation. "Why didn't one of you tell me? I looked up and you were driving off."

"She didn't want to ruin Matt and Stephanie's moment."

"That doesn't explain why you didn't come get me," he gritted out.

"You were busy talking to Starla," A.J. pointed out. "Toni didn't want to make a scene so she asked me to take her home."

Anger and fear built within him as he watched Toni anxiously talk on the phone. Her fear reached out to him. He could practically feel it from here. Why hadn't she told him? Were they getting so far apart? What in the world was happening to them?

When she put the phone down, he immediately went to her side. "What did he say?" he demanded.

She looked questioningly up at A.J.

"I told him," A.J. explained.

"Why didn't *you* tell me?" Simon asked.

"I didn't want to worry you," she said softly.

"Too late. Now what did the doctor tell you. Do we need to take you to the hospital?"

She looked up at him, her brown eyes filled with uncertainty. "He said to lie down and take it easy. If I continue to spot or if I start having contractions, he wants me to go into the hospital. But otherwise, he wants me on bed rest for the rest of the day."

"Is there something I can do?" he asked helplessly.

She shook her head and started to rise. He caught her hand, feeling her tremble. "Want me to get you a pillow and blanket so you can lay down right here?"

She smiled and he felt something within him start to melt. "I'd like that. Thanks."

He went to the closet and pulled out two pillows and a blanket then returned to the couch. He plumped the pillows and set them on the end then he patted it, gesturing for her to lie down. As she settled on the couch, he pulled the blanket up over her. He let his hand drift to her cheek to smooth the tendrils of hair from her face. Her skin felt velvety soft under his fingertips and he resisted the temptation to touch her lips.

He yanked his hand away and mentally shook himself. "Get some rest, sweetheart."

Turning away, he met A.J.'s gaze and motioned him into the kitchen. "Can you take Steve's truck back to the barbeque and get him to run you back home? He let me borrow it to run home, and I thought I'd just get you to follow me back in mine, but I don't want to leave Toni alone."

"Yeah sure," A.J. said, reaching for the keys.

Toni watched from the couch as Simon turned and walked over to her once more. She smiled tentatively up at him as he knelt by the couch. "How you doing? Any cramping?" he asked.

"You've been reading my pregnancy book again," she said with a laugh. But she found it endearing he had devoted so much time to reading about something that affected her.

She reached a hand up and placed it on his chest. "Thank you," she whispered.

"For what?" he asked, confusion clouding his eyes.

"For caring about me," she said softly.

Not taking the time to ponder whether this was the appropriate moment, she smoothed her hand up over his shoulder and over the back of his neck. Pulling him down at the same time she raised her lips, she pressed her mouth to his.

He stiffened in surprise, but she moved her lips softly over his, seeking, almost pleading with him to respond. His mouth opened, and he took control of the kiss. His hand slid up to her neck holding her against him as his tongue darted forth.

She moaned softly, twining her fingers in his hair pulling him even closer. Heaven had nothing on Simon. His kiss was possessive, strong, everything she'd dreamed about since their first night together. Only now he knew what he was doing.

A giddy thrill shot through her body as the kiss went on, his hot breath on her face only fanning the out of control flames.

Then he jerked away leaving her struggling to catch her breath. His eyes were bright with...regret? Shock? He rocked back on his heels and ran a hand through his hair, then swore.

This wasn't the reaction she'd envisioned.

She struggled to sit up, wrapping her arms around her chest in a protective measure. Then she waited with dread for him to speak.

"Jesus, Toni. I'm sorry. Christ, are you okay?"

She nodded, too numb to speak. He was apologizing. Humiliation edged every bit of the euphoria that had swept over her just seconds ago. Slow heat spread up her neck and over her cheeks. "I'm fine," she finally murmured.

Not saying anything further, she rose, wrapping her dignity around her like a tattered blanket then walked through the kitchen toward her room.

"Toni, wait," he called.

Ignoring his plea, she quietly closed the door behind her and locked it. If she didn't get out of there soon, she was going to lose all semblance of self control.

The tears came before she got to her bed. She knew it was a long shot, but hope springs eternal. Or it did. Now she was going to have to face the music. She was pregnant and alone. Simon didn't see her as anything more than a kid sister. The sooner she came to terms with that the sooner she could get on with her future. Single motherhood.

Her doorknob jiggled then a soft knock sounded. "Toni? Toni, open the door please. We need to talk. God, I'm sorry. I had no right to do that."

She buried her head further into her pillow and shut out the sound of his pleading. After a few minutes, she could hear him walk away.

She rolled onto her side and gripped the pillow against her chest. What the hell was she going to do? She couldn't face him now. Once again, she'd screwed up royally. And this time she'd probably ruined their friendship as well.

In a few months, she'd be moving out. That much was known. But what to do in the meantime? She had to start thinking of her future in terms that didn't include Simon. As painful as it was, it was time to face the cold hard facts.

She didn't have a college degree. She was pregnant. She wasn't married. Three things working against her.

She had a great job considering her lack of a degree, but it wasn't enough to foot the bill for the upcoming days. So what could she do about it? There wasn't time to devote to going back to school. She needed the additional income now, not later.

She heard the door slam and tensed, waiting to see if anyone would come to her door. Would Simon tell Matt and A.J. what happened? Surely not. But the thought made her nauseous.

How could she face any of them? And what a complete cluster fuck she had made of her life. It would be a miracle if she managed to have a normal child.

She needed to figure out where to get a job. She could work a few nights a week and maybe weekends until the baby came. The extra money would come in handy when she had to pay for her own place and daycare for the baby.

She had some money in savings. Money she'd received when her parents died. But now it had to be reserved for her child's future.

Who was she kidding? She was getting a job because it would keep her away from Simon. Yeah, she was a coward. And she *did* need the money. She had things to buy. Baby furniture. A crib and cute little clothes. And while she was at it, she had to figure out what to do about the little matter of the baby's father.

Simon sat at the bar staring out the kitchen window. Toni had refused to open her door, and he was feeling more miserable by the minute. Having his testicles forcibly removed with a rusty knife was too good for him at the moment.

What kind of clod was he to have taken advantage of Toni at her weakest moment? She'd been spotting. She was scared to death to lose her baby, and all he could think about was how good she tasted, how smooth her skin felt beneath his touch, and how he wanted nothing more than to make love to her all night long.

He looked up as Matt and A.J. drove up, cringing at the thought of telling them what he had done. Then again, he wasn't stupid. Better to keep his mouth shut.

Matt walked in, worry evident in his eyes. "Where's Toni?"

Simon gestured toward the bedroom. "She went to bed," he muttered.

"Was she doing okay?" Matt persisted.

"Yeah, I think so. She talked to her doc and he didn't sound too concerned. Just wanted her to take it easy."

"It's good she went to bed," A.J. said. "I'm sure bonehead falling on her today had a lot to do with the spotting."

Simon scowled at the mention of Mike. "He doesn't watch out for her like he should."

"I have to agree with you there," Matt said, nodding his head slowly. "I don't know what she sees in him to be honest. I'm tempted to have a talk with her."

"Maybe so. You're her brother after all," A.J. spoke up. "Maybe you can talk some sense into her."

"I think she's having a hard time right now," Matt said regretfully. "I feel to blame. I'm not sure it was the right time to talk about marriage with Steph."

Simon remained silent, not agreeing or disagreeing with that sentiment. In truth, he did agree that the timing was rotten. He had no doubt Toni was dealing with a lot. Adapting to her pregnancy not to mention moving out of the house she'd called home since she was child. He wanted to be angry with Matt, but he couldn't begrudge him his happiness.

"I'm heading to bed," he announced, unable to stand it any longer. The kiss was haunting him. He had replayed it over and over in his head until it became one continuous stream.

He said goodnight and went straight to the bathroom. He needed a shower. A very cold shower.

Chapter Fourteen

After a sleepless night, Toni got up and showered. She had gotten up several times during the night, checking to see if she was still spotting. To her relief, there had been no evidence of blood and she'd experienced no cramping.

The guys were late sleepers, and if she was lucky, she'd be able to get out of the house without getting a lecture on staying in bed or encountering Simon.

A flush crawled over her face at the idea of looking Simon in the eye. His apology was too fresh on her mind, and the look of horror in his face when she'd kissed him was enough to make her want to keep her distance for a while.

She tiptoed out of her room, relieved to see the kitchen empty. She froze when she saw Simon asleep on the couch. Had he waited up for her? Acting quickly, she scribbled a note and left it out on the bar so they guys wouldn't worry. She poured a glass of juice to take with her and headed back out to her Jeep.

The first order of business was to find a part time job. She had a few ideas and would check them out before she got desperate enough to go flip burgers. Lonnie Bristow, the head of Emergency Medical Services dispatch had offered her a job before when she'd filled in one summer. Perhaps he needed a PRN person.

She drove to central dispatch, just two blocks from the fire station and the county run ambulance service. Luck was with her and Lonnie was in his office.

He looked up when she knocked and smiled welcomingly. "Hey Toni. Come on in. What can I do for you?"

"Hi, Lonnie." She slid into a chair in front of his desk and nervously took in a breath. "I was wondering if you had any PRN positions open."

He raised his eyebrow in surprise. "Sure. I always need dispatchers to fill in. As it is, most people are working extra hours. You asking for yourself?"

She nodded. "I still work for Doc Johnson so I could only work weekends or in the evenings, but I'd like the part time work."

"I sure won't turn down an experienced dispatcher." He rolled back in his chair to the file cabinet behind him and rifled through one of the drawers. He pulled out an application and handed it to her. "Fill this out and get it back to me. When would you like to start?"

"As soon as possible," she replied, taking the paper from him.

He handed her a pen and studied her for a moment. "I've known you for a long time, Toni. What's going on? Are you in some kind of trouble?"

She raised her eyes to look at him. "Oh no. No trouble. I'm sure you've heard by now." She paused a moment. He hadn't been at the barbeque, but as much as the town loved to gossip, she couldn't imagine he hadn't heard.

"Heard what?"

"That I'm pregnant. I just need the extra money until the baby's born."

He tried to mask the surprise, but his eyes gave him away. "No, I hadn't heard. Congratulations."

"Thank you. You're the first person to actually congratulate me and mean it," she said with a smile.

"I can well imagine," he said dryly.

She handed the application back to him.

He glanced over it a moment, then looked at his calendar. "Want to come in Monday after you get off work and reacquaint yourself with the surroundings? Sarah is working then, and she'll be glad to show you the ropes again."

"That would be great." She got up and extended her hand. "Thank, Lonnie. I owe you one."

"Hell no you don't. If you only knew how badly I needed dispatchers. I should be down kissing your feet."

She grinned. "I'll see you Monday then."

Feeling a little lighter, she got into her Jeep and checked her watch. It was only ten. Well, now that she had another job, she could go look for baby things anyway. And it sure beat going back home and facing Simon.

Tomorrow she'd run her job idea by her doctor and get his okay before she committed to the whole shebang. She needed the job. Needed the money. *Needed* to get away from Simon before she imploded. But she would do nothing at the expense of her baby. Their baby.

🚒 🚒 🚒

By seven, she was thoroughly exhausted. She'd hit every department store in Beaumont, not to mention every baby boutique and furniture store. Her list had been compiled of exactly what she wanted. A crib small enough to fit in her bedroom. A bassinet for the living room. Lots of must haves, according to the saleswoman, like a swing and bouncer.

Unable to avoid the inevitable any longer, she turned homeward, praying that A.J. and Matt were at home so she could avoid any conversation with Simon. All three trucks were in the driveway to her relief. She parked then trudged into the house.

Three sets of eyes stared at her when she opened the door. Her fatigue must have been evident because they immediately pounced.

"Where the hell have you been all day?" Matt demanded. "You look like hell."

"I'm tired. I'm going to bed." She started toward her room, avoiding Simon's gaze when A.J. spoke up.

"Is everything okay, Toni?"

She smiled crookedly. "Yeah, just overdid it. G'night."

Not waiting for them to say anything more, she escaped to her room and locked the door behind her. No sooner had she gotten undressed and into bed a knock sounded at her door.

"Toni, it's me Matt."

"I'm in bed," she called.

"I want to talk to you."

"Can it wait? I'm really tired."

There was a long pause. "Okay. Get some rest. We'll talk later."

She laid back and closed her eyes. Then the tears fell.

🚒 🚒 🚒

Monday she congratulated herself on going the entire weekend without seeing Simon more than in passing. She'd work in dispatch after work and the guys were starting a forty-eight on Tuesday, so the earliest she'd see Simon would be Thursday afternoon. Provided she didn't work that night.

She got off a little early so she went home to change before she headed in to her second job. When she let herself in, the guys were all watching TV in the living room. She called out a hello then went into her bedroom to change.

Moments later she came back out and paused in the kitchen. Knowing she had to at least tell them where she was going, she cleared her throat. "I'll see you guys later."

They swiveled around to look at her. "Where you going?" A.J. asked.

"Work." The word hung in the air a moment as they digested what she'd said.

"Work?" Matt asked. "You just got home from work."

"I'm doing some PRN work for Lonnie over at dispatch."

Their surprise was evident. "Huh? Since when?" Matt asked.

"Since Saturday."

"Hell, Toni, you used to tell us shit like this. What's the deal lately?" Matt's voice rose, and he got up to walk toward her. "You should be in bed resting. Have you forgotten what happened a few days ago?"

"Look it's no big deal. I just haven't seen you guys what with your schedules lately. I gotta run, or I'll be late. I'll talk to you later." She blew a kiss at Matt and spun around to leave.

Simon watched her walk out and suppressed the urge to put his fist through the coffee table. It didn't take a rocket scientist to figure out she was avoiding him.

Matt returned to the living room a deep frown on his face. "I don't know what the hell is going on with her, but she isn't telling us something."

"Oh you think?" A.J. muttered.

"What's with her getting a second job? She's pregnant for Christ sake. She doesn't need to be working two jobs," Matt said in a raised voice. He turned to Simon. "You usually aren't short on something to say. Do you know what's eating Toni?"

Yeah he knew all right. But he wasn't going to blurt out that he'd been putting the moves on Toni in her weak moment. Matt and A.J. would use his face for a punching bag. "No, I don't. Maybe she just needed the extra cash with the baby coming."

Matt snorted. "There's no way in hell I'd let her work two jobs when she's pregnant. If it's money she needs, she only has to ask."

"But that's just it," Simon said. "I don't see her asking anyone for anything. You know as well as I do, she'd never do anything she thought would make herself a burden."

"I think it's something else," A.J. popped up. "I don't know what it is…yet. But I aim to find out."

🚒 🚒 🚒

Nothing had changed in dispatch since she'd last worked, and she picked up the mechanics again quickly. She sat for a few hours watching and listening to Sarah and Cody, the other dispatcher.

When she was ready to leave, Sarah pulled her aside. "First of all, I wanted to offer my congratulations on the baby."

"Thanks, Sarah. I appreciate it." Sarah was a down to earth woman in her thirties. She had a no-nonsense approach to everything, and next to Lonnie, she called the shots around dispatch.

"Secondly, Lonnie figured you'd pick things back up quickly so he left a tentative schedule for you. Look over it and see what you think. If it's okay, we'll jot you down for those days."

Toni took the sheet from her and glanced over it. She worked both days of the upcoming weekend, plus one weeknight in between. The rest of the month consisted of at least one weekend day and two to three weeknights. Not overwhelming, but it sure wouldn't leave much time at home. It was perfect.

"These are fine," she said handing back the schedule to Sarah.

"You sure it won't be too much with you being pregnant?"

"I'll be fine. I can always sit with my feet up."

"That's true," Sarah said with a grin. "I'll make sure Lonnie gets you a nice cushion. You could probably ask for just about anything at this point. He's so grateful he'd likely give it to you."

Toni laughed. "I'll keep that in mind."

"Well, you get on home. I'll see you Thursday."

Toni waved and headed out to her Jeep. When she got home and let herself in the house, she nearly groaned aloud. Matt, A.J. and Simon were all sitting on the couch obviously waiting for her.

Ignoring them, she set about making a sandwich.

"It's not going to work," Matt announced.

She turned around and raised her brow.

"You're ignoring us."

"I'm eating," she pointed out.

"Well, that's something, at least. You haven't been doing enough of that lately."

"Don't lecture," she said with a frown. She turned back to her sandwich, but she felt their stares. If she were really brave, she'd go to her room and bar the door. But that would immediately send the signal she was indeed avoiding them. Better to sit here and eat then go to bed.

"We want to talk to you, Toni," Matt persisted.

With a sigh she turned back around. "Can a girl eat in peace?"

"By all means finish, but when you're done, we're going to have a little talk."

She rolled her eyes. "There's nothing to talk about."

"I think there is," Simon spoke up, his voice strained.

Panic assailed her. Surely he wouldn't bring up what happened in front of the guys. Her food coiled in a knot in her throat then hit her stomach like a ton of bricks. Her stomach lurched in protest.

Not bothering to explain, she bolted for the bathroom. Her stomach emptied in short order. She leaned heavily against the toilet, anxiety eating a hole in her gut.

"Toni, open the damn door," Matt demanded.

Well, at least it wasn't Simon. Weakly, she flipped the bolt then returned to her stance of hanging her head over the bowl.

"Are you okay?" he asked as he shoved into the small bathroom with her.

"Yeah, I'm fine."

He grabbed a washcloth from the closet and ran cold water over it. "Here," he said offering it to her.

"Thanks." She rose slowly, wiping her forehead with the cloth.

"Now suppose you tell me what the hell is going on with you."

She flushed the toilet then lowered the seat so she could sit. "Nothing is going on. This is normal pregnancy stuff."

"I see. You getting a second job is normal pregnancy stuff. And not saying anything to me about it is normal pregnancy stuff." He crossed his arms over his chest and stared hard at her.

She let out a frustrated sigh. "It's no big deal. I wanted the extra money for when the baby comes. Lonnie's offered me a job before. I thought it would be a great job. You worked on Sunday so I didn't see you."

"You used to come around the station," he pointed out. "And in the past you would have come right over to share any news."

"I just don't feel comfortable coming around right now," she hedged. It wasn't a complete lie. She was uncomfortable, but her pregnancy had nothing to do with it.

"Is my asking Stephanie to marry me bothering you? You know I wouldn't do anything to hurt you, Toni. If you want to stay here, just say so. I don't want you killing yourself at a second job in order to afford to move out."

She stared at him in shock. "No. God, no. That isn't it at all, Matt. I'm thrilled for you. Stephanie is a wonderful girl and you deserve to be happy. I'm angry at myself for being such a screwup. You shouldn't have to plan your life around me and my stupidity."

He frowned hard at her. "I don't want to ever hear you talking like that. Stephanie and I could never be happy knowing it was at your expense. And you aren't stupid. No one thinks that."

"So you don't think it's stupid I got myself knocked up and have no man in the wings?" she asked dryly. She immediately regretted her snappy question when Matt jumped on it with both feet.

"I have to admit I'm curious," he said quietly. "You've never talked about the father. I've respected your privacy, but I'm a little hurt you feel you can't confide in me."

She groaned. "Oh, Matt. It's not that I can't confide in you. The fact is I can't confide in anyone right now. I've just got to work out some things on my own."

"I don't like this distance I feel opening up between you and us. You know A.J. and Simon love you as much as I do. We're family."

Her heart constricted. Matt would be so pissed if she ruined things between the four of them. And she may well have already done it.

"Just give me some time. This pregnancy gig isn't a cake walk."

"Let us help you, Toni. You aren't alone."

"Thanks, Matt. I just need some time to sort things out."

"Okay, I'll back off, but you have to promise to take it easy. I don't like this second job you've gotten at all. And if you don't take care of yourself, I'll make sure Lonnie cans your ass."

She laughed. "Okay, deal. Now if you don't mind, I'm going to bed."

He gave her a hug and kissed her forehead. "I'll see you on Thursday."

She wasn't about to tell him she worked then. After he'd left, she shuffled into her bedroom and pulled back the covers. Truth was, she didn't feel much like going to sleep, but the alternative was getting the riot act from the guys.

Chapter Fifteen

Thursday morning, to her surprise, she seemed to have popped out overnight. When she shed her clothes to get into the shower, she had a very noticeable bulge. She stood in front of the mirror examining all the different angles.

According to her pregnancy book, she should have already felt the baby's first kick. She'd worried over it at first, but her doctor had assured her everything was progressing just fine.

After she dressed, she surveyed her appearance one more time. She grinned. Yep, there was no mistaking her pregnancy now. "Now if you would only let me know you're in there," she said smoothing her hands over the bulge.

Before she left, she wrote a note saying she was working that night and left it out on the counter.

The day passed quickly. At five, she changed her clothes at the veterinary practice then headed over to dispatch. Sarah walked in just as she sat down to don her headphones. She motioned for Toni to take them off. "Call this your baptism by fire, but can you work tomorrow night? I know you're scheduled for the weekend, but Cody's out sick and Steven's mother died so he's going to be out of town for a week at least. I wondered if you could take over a half shift for the next ten days."

"Sure," Toni replied.

"You feel up to it?"

"I'm pregnant, not dying of a terminal illness," she retorted.

"Fair enough. Okay then, I'll see you every day at five thirty. Except this weekend. I need you here at eight to work a full shift if you can."

Toni nodded and put her headphones back on.

At eleven, she drove home ready to fall into bed. It wasn't strenuous work, but coupled with a long day at the veterinary clinic, it became interminable. What had she gotten herself into by agreeing to work the next ten days straight?

Simon and A.J. were up watching TV when she came in. They immediately got up when they heard her. "How was work?" A.J. asked as he ambled into the kitchen.

Simon slid onto a barstool and watched her across the table. His gaze made her uncomfortable so she concentrated on A.J. "It was fine. Not much going on tonight. A fire over on Stiller road. Turns out old Mrs. Studdard left one of her cigars burning. Caught her drapes on fire."

A.J. laughed. "Glad I wasn't working tonight."

She turned to put her glass in the sink when she felt a light fluttering in her stomach. She gasped and her hand flew to the bump.

From nowhere, Simon was beside her. "Are you all right?" He gripped her arms with his hands. "What's wrong?"

She smiled, a feeling of awe pouring over her. "Nothing. I mean it's just the baby. It kicked."

"Cool!" A.J. exclaimed.

"Where?" Simon asked softly putting a hand over her stomach.

"Here." She slid his hand over the slight bumping on her left side.

A peculiar expression lit his face. "That's amazing."

"Let me feel," A.J. said, pushing Simon aside.

He put his hand over her stomach and waited. A few seconds later the tiny bumping resumed. "Wow. That's weird."

She laughed. "Weird? Well, I guess so. It feels even weirder."

"It's like that alien movie where the alien bursts out of the woman's stomach. Freaky."

"You watch way too much TV," Simon muttered.

"I'm going to say goodnight now," she announced. "I'll see you guys later."

Simon's look of frustration told her he had been waiting up to talk to her. More the reason for her to get out of Dodge quick.

🚒 🚒 🚒

"I'm going to kill Lonnie," Simon muttered as he and A.J. threw their gear into their lockers.

"Dare I ask why?" A.J. asked with a raised brow.

"He's working Toni way too hard. Hell, she hasn't had a night off since she started working there almost two weeks ago. She's exhausted. She's working herself into the ground."

"Yeah, last time I saw her, she wasn't looking too great. That was a few days ago, so I can't imagine she's looking any better now."

Simon glanced over at him. "What do you mean? She looks great. She's just tired."

A.J. laughed. "Calm down. I didn't say she needed a paper bag over her head. And yeah, she looks very tired." He glanced over at Simon, his look of amusement gone. "So tell me. What happened between the two of you?"

The knot grew bigger in Simon's stomach. A.J. had always been too perceptive for his own good. "I don't know what you're talking about."

A.J. snorted. "Please. I'm not an idiot. She's avoiding us all like the plague, but you in particular."

He rubbed his face in agitation. "Yeah well, she has reason."

A.J. leaned back against his locker. "What'd you do?"

"I kissed her."

A.J.'s lips twitched suspiciously. "She's avoiding you because you kissed her?"

"Not exactly. I was a jerk. I took advantage of her."

"This I gotta hear."

When he finished telling A.J. the whole story, A.J. dissolved into laughter.

"I'm glad you find it so funny," he muttered.

"Simon, for such an intelligent, serious guy you can be such a moron sometimes."

"What's that supposed to mean?"

"First of all, you said she kissed you."

"Well, she did. But I doubt she realized what she was doing. And I didn't have to respond."

A.J. shook his head. "Uh huh. Does Toni strike you as the helpless female who doesn't have a clue what she's doing?"

He frowned. "Well, no."

"Ding ding ding. We have a winner."

"Shut the hell up," he growled. "What are you getting at? Do you think she kissed me on purpose?"

"Well, unless she thought in her delirium that you were me, and she has a mega crush on me, then yeah, I'd say she meant to kiss you."

"Then why is she avoiding me?"

"Hmmm, good question. What did you do after she kissed you?"

Heat rushed his cheeks as he remembered with great detail exactly what he'd done. How good she'd felt. And how much he'd fantasized about doing it again. He cleared his throat. "I, uh, kissed her back."

"Yeah, and then what."

"I came to my senses and jerked away. Then I apologized."

He reared back when A.J. smacked him on the head. "What the hell was that for?"

"Idiot. And you wonder why she's avoiding you."

"I don't get it."

"I think that year with Starla addled your brains. You can't have always been this stupid about women."

"Would you quit with the insults and tell me what the hell you're talking about?"

"You apologized. In other words, you told her, not only by your action of pulling away, but by your apology that you regretted it happening. That translates to a woman as he doesn't want me. Doesn't find me attractive."

"You're telling me, she's pissed because she thinks I don't want her?"

"Uh huh. And they say you're the bright one."

He sank down onto the bench. Did that mean she was attracted to him? "Are you saying Toni has a thing for me?"

"Look dude, the way I see it she put everything on the line and you totally shot her down. In her position, I don't think I'd be lining up for casual conversation either."

"Shit."

"So tell me. How'd you feel about the kiss?"

"I've never experienced anything like it," he said honestly.

"So what's the problem?"

"The problem is I don't want to screw up the dynamics of a really great friendship. I have more to consider than just whether things go sour between me and Toni. What happens between us directly affects the four of us."

"Matt and I are big boys. The question you have to ask yourself is whether you've screwed up things by not acting."

"So you think I should pursue her?"

"I don't think anything. What do you want? Are you attracted to her?"

"I've thought of little else than making love to her for the past month," he admitted in a rush. He glanced up to gauge A.J.'s reaction to his outburst.

A.J. grinned. "Gotten under you skin eh?"

"You could say that."

"Aside from wanting to get her in the sack, how do you feel about her?"

He looked at A.J. like he'd grown a third head. "If you're asking if I just want a one night stand with her I might punch you in the teeth. I'd never treat her that way."

"If I thought you only wanted a one-nighter with her I'd punch *you* in the teeth. Stop worrying so much about everyone else and think about what's best for you and Toni. The way I see it you couldn't ask for a better girl. And she needs someone right now. If she's interested in you then you are one lucky guy. But if you don't get off your ass and do something about it, you're going to lose out on the best thing that'll ever happen to you."

He turned and sauntered out of the locker room, leaving Simon to ponder their conversation. Was A.J. right? Could Toni be attracted to him? Had he hurt her by pushing her away?

He got up and punched the locker with a loud bang. What was holding him back? The truth was he cared a lot for Toni. And not in a little sibling capacity. But it would kill him to lose her if things didn't work out.

But it looked as if he'd lose her by doing nothing. He needed to talk to Matt. Tell him what had happened and that he was going to pursue a relationship with Toni. This had to be handled carefully or the lives of four people could change for the worse.

He walked into the lounge searching out Matt among the group of firemen. "Can I talk to you?" he asked when he found Matt in the kitchen.

"Sure, what's up?"

"Not here. Let's go in the garage."

Matt gave him a curious look but followed behind.

"Something wrong?" he asked when the two were alone.

"No, not wrong. I just wanted to talk to you about something. Give you a heads up so to speak."

"Okay."

He paused for a moment then looked Matt straight in the eye. "I'm interested in Toni."

Matt's eyes popped open wide. "Whoa. I had no idea."

"Yeah, well I think she might be interested in me as well. I wanted you to know because I don't want anything to mess up our friendship."

Matt frowned slightly. "What makes you think she's interested in you?"

Leave it to Matt to want specifics. "We, uh, kissed awhile back. I screwed things up which is why Toni's avoiding us. Me in particular."

"If you want my blessing, you've got it. I can't imagine a better couple. But I think you've got a difficult road ahead. I mean she *is* pregnant. Are you prepared for that kind of responsibility?"

"I don't know all of that yet," he admitted. "This isn't something I ever expected would happen. We'll have to take things a day at a time and see what happens. No matter what though, I'll always be there to help her."

"You'll also have to figure out who the father is. I mean, you can't exactly have a solid relationship until you find out if this guy's going to be in the picture or not."

Simon frowned. The idea of another man making love to Toni twisted his insides. He wouldn't pressure her, but if they were going to become involved, the subject would have to come up. The main obstacle now, however, was convincing her to talk to him about their own relationship.

Chapter Sixteen

Two weeks. Two miserable, long weeks. She was tired, and she was lonely. She glanced over the schedule and rubbed her eyes wearily. Thank God today was a relatively light patient load. She was even more thankful it was Friday, and she didn't have to work the next day.

Her plan to avoid Simon had worked too well. She missed him. And she'd come to the realization she'd been a royal twit. So what if he wasn't falling at her feet. He was the best friend she'd ever have besides A.J., and there was no way in hell she'd spend the rest of her pregnancy in solitude.

She determined the first time she saw him she'd beg his forgiveness and blame the whole episode on pregnancy hormones. Hell, if hormones were a defense for murder, they may as well be an excuse for throwing yourself at a hunky guy.

Glancing down at the desk, she resisted the urge to lay her head down on it. One more night at work then she could sleep as late as she wanted tomorrow.

Her head was nearly to the desk when the bell on the door sounded, and she jerked back up. She blinked in surprise to see Simon standing in front of her, a determined look on his face.

"Simon. Uh, what are you doing here?"

He strode over behind the desk. "We need to talk, and I'm tired of you avoiding me."

"But I…" Her words trailed off. No need in denying it since that was precisely what she'd been doing.

"Is there some place we can go? One of the exam rooms maybe?"

"Uh, sure, just a sec. I need to let Marnie know so she can watch the front." She gestured for him to follow her down the hallway, then opened one of the surgical prep rooms. "I'll be right back."

Her heart racing, she went in search of Marnie and asked her to mind the front for a few minutes. She returned to where Simon waited and nervously wiped her palms on her lab coat before going in. She shut the door behind her and looked cautiously at him.

Not giving her a chance to say anything, he closed the distance between them. With one swift motion, he pulled her into his arms and covered her lips with his. Her mouth fell open in a gasp of surprise. His tongue took advantage and darted forward, tracing the edges of her lips then delving between them teasing her tongue with his.

He buried one hand in her long hair and brought his other arm around her waist pulling her against his hard chest. Of all the things she thought he might have done, this wasn't one of them.

When he released her, she stepped back, her lips still tingling from his assault on her senses.

"That's in case you think I didn't want you the last time we kissed," he said, his eyes fiery with…desire? Did he want her as badly as she wanted him?

She opened her mouth to speak, but honestly couldn't summon any words. What could she say after all?

He cupped her chin in his hand and gently kissed her once again. "I've wanted to do that for the longest time."

"Then why didn't you?" she blurted. Her cheeks flamed at her outburst.

He smiled a slow sexy smile. "Good question. But I plan to make up for lost time."

She gulped. "I don't understand."

He ran a hand through his hair and started pacing in front of her. "I know I probably hurt you with the way I reacted last time, and I'm sorry. I honestly didn't know how the hell to act. I wanted you badly, had wanted you for quite awhile, and suddenly you kissed me. I felt like a toad for taking advantage of you when you were vulnerable. And," he said after a long pause. "I didn't want to screw up our friendship."

She stared at him open-mouthed. She knew she must look ridiculous gaping at him like an idiot, but she couldn't comprehend what was happening. Here was Simon admitting he was attracted to her. He laid a kiss on her that had curled every single one of her toes, and all she could do was stand, speechless.

"Now, I've laid my cards on the table," he murmured, stroking a hand through her hair. "Now suppose you tell me why you kissed me."

"Couldn't you kiss me again and forget about talking?" she asked hopefully.

He chuckled and dipped his head to kiss her lips. In between kisses he said, "I have no qualms about kissing you again, but it isn't going to get you out of answering me."

"Mmmm," she murmured against his lips.

He drew away slowly, his eyes half lidded. "Now, talk to me."

Feeling a bit more confident now that she had the man of her dreams showering her with kisses, she cleared her throat. "I've had the biggest crush on you forever. I've been doing everything I can think of to get you to notice me, and until now thought I'd failed miserably."

"You little minx. Do you mean to tell me the sexy lingerie, the braless T-shirt, that was all for my benefit?"

She blushed. "Yes. Mike gave me the ideas."

He nearly choked and dissolved into a coughing fit. "Wait a minute. You mean to tell me Mike was coaching you on how to seduce me?"

"Uh, yeah."

"I don't know whether to be flattered or insulted," he said with a shake of his head.

"Well I had to do something," she said defensively. "I didn't know how to make you see me as anything more than a little sister."

"You certainly succeeded," he murmured. "Now that we have this settled, I have plans for us for the weekend. Starting as soon as you get off from work."

She looked regretfully at him. "I have to work dispatch tonight."

"Not anymore," he said in a smug tone. "I cleared it with Lonnie. You have the night off and you don't go back to work until next Wednesday. You need the time off. You aren't taking care of yourself and I plan to remedy that this weekend."

Liquid heat curled in her stomach and spread into her chest. A huge silly grin fought to break out of her lips. She had the insane urge to twirl round and round in delight. And once again reality crashed in.

She still had to tell him about the baby.

"Why the frown?" he asked in concern.

"Oh nothing," she said brightly. "A weekend off sounds heavenly. What do you have in mind?"

He waggled his eyebrows suggestively. "You'll see." He leaned over to kiss her once more, his lips lingering on hers for a long moment. "I'll see you in an hour at the house. Don't be late." He smiled and walked out of the door.

Toni sagged against the counter. Holy moly, that man was sex in a jar. A giddy thrill washed through her and she succumbed to the desire to do a victory dance.

She bopped out to the front where Marnie was sitting, a wide grim nearly splitting her face in two.

"What's got you so chipper?" Marnie asked giving her a speculative glance.

"You just saw the sexiest man who ever lived go through that door," she said, easing into the chair beside Marnie.

The older woman's eyes twinkled. "I thought he might have something to do with that spring in your step. It's about time you landed that young man."

"Oh, I haven't landed him yet. But I've definitely got him on the hook. Now if I can just reel him in."

On the way home she thanked God there weren't any cops out because she was exceeding the speed limit by a good ten miles an hour.

When she pulled into the drive she saw all three trucks there and frowned. Somehow A.J. and Matt being there hadn't fit with her expectation of the evening.

When she walked in, she was immediately met by Simon who planted a kiss on her lips. "Hey gorgeous," he said in a husky voice.

A ridiculously large smile burst forth from her lips.

"Now that's more like it," he said guiding her into the kitchen. "I haven't seen you smile like that in weeks."

Matt and A.J. were in the kitchen doing something that suspiciously resembled cooking. She glanced questioningly at them and A.J. grinned. "Never let it be said I don't love you. I'm slaving over a hot stove in your honor."

"What's going on?" she asked Simon as he ushered her onto a stool.

"You've been overdoing it, and tonight we're going to wait on you hand and foot. That is if knuckle head over there hasn't managed to burn dinner."

"I resemble that remark," A.J. joked.

Matt set a plate in front of her and a tall glass of tea.

"You guys didn't have to do this," she protested.

"Don't worry," A.J. said leaning over and whispering in a conspiratorial voice. "Matt and I are leaving after dinner."

Her cheeks flamed, and A.J. laughed and returned to the stove.

Moments later, he and Matt served up a plate of steaming spaghetti and fresh rolls. They talked over dinner, and for the first time in several weeks, the easy rapport between them all was back.

After dinner, Matt and A.J. cleared away the dishes then made a big show of going out. When they'd gone, Simon guided Toni to the couch and made her sit down. He eased down beside her and put an arm around her back. "Now that they are gone, I thought you could spend a nice relaxing evening. You're dead on your feet."

"I am tired," she admitted.

"Tomorrow I'd like to take you out on a real date."

She smiled up at him. "I'd like that."

He caught her lips with his and gently cupped her cheek in his palm. She sighed in utter contentment and lost herself in his touch. When he drew away, she rested her head on his chest, snuggling against his warmth. "Can I ask you something?"

"Sure, anything," his chest rumbled against her ear as he replied

"When did you become attracted to me?"

"Hmmm well, I think the first time I really took notice was the night Starla and I broke up."

She stiffened against him, her heart swelling in panic.

"I remember thinking all women should be more like you. Honest, understanding, supportive, straightforward."

"You make me sound like a faithful dog," she said in amusement.

"I mean it as the sincerest compliment."

She pulled away and looked up at him. "What about Starla? Are you two still seeing each other?"

A shuttered look fell over his face. "We aren't seeing each other. I mean we aren't dating. I've seen her a couple of times just to talk, but there's nothing between us anymore."

Unease fell over her as she witnessed his discomfort. Did he still have feelings for her? He'd dated Starla for a long time. Had even been ready to propose to her. It had to have been hard to get over her that quickly.

"Let's talk about something else," he said. "How about when you decided you were attracted to me."

"That's easy," she muttered. "Only for bloody ever."

"Really?"

"Yeah," she sighed.

She leaned forward to kick off her shoes and rubbed one of her feet in a soothing gesture.

"Here, let me," he offered, rearranging himself on the couch so he held her feet in his lap. He began massaging the souls and working his way up to the instep.

She moaned in sheer bliss. Leaning back against the arm, she closed her eyes and gave herself over to the exquisite pleasure of the foot rub.

Her eyes fluttered drowsily as she succumbed to her fatigue.

Simon looked up to see she'd fallen asleep while he rubbed her feet. He smiled and continued massaging for a few minutes then he gently lowered her feet off his lap.

Quietly, so as not to disturb her, he got up and retrieved a blanket from the hall closet. He eased it over her and tucked her in. He stood and watched the even rise and fall of her chest for a long time. One thing was certain. If she was going to be his, he'd make damn sure she took better care of herself.

Chapter Seventeen

Toni woke and stretched languidly. The living room ceiling came into focus, and her brow furrowed as she tried to remember how she'd gotten on the couch. The last thing she remembered was getting a foot rub that rivaled any thing she'd ever experienced.

"Good morning, sleepyhead." Simon's face came into view. He carried a tray that he set on the coffee table in front of the couch.

She sat up, the blanket falling to her waist. "Smells good."

"Eat up. We're leaving in an hour."

She arched an eyebrow. "Where we going?"

"How does a day at the beach sound? I packed us lunch. We can take the ferry across to Galveston and back, then enjoy a walk along the surf."

Despite being Fall, the Texas coast was mild. It had been several months since she'd ventured down to the beach, and she couldn't think of anything nicer than watching the sunset with Simon. She eagerly nodded her agreement and took the tray he offered.

After she ate the eggs, bacon and toast, she downed the glass of juice and rose from the couch to go shower. A half hour later she walked back into the kitchen wearing maternity jeans and one of her new maternity tops.

"You ready to go?" Simon asked as he collected the cooler from the bar.

She nodded and they walked out to his truck. After putting the cooler in back, he opened the door for her then walked around to the driver's seat. He paused a moment before starting the engine and looked over at her. "Here's to our first official date."

She ducked her head, knowing she was grinning like a fool.

The drove down interstate ten toward Houston. The bright blue autumn sky was unmarred by a single cloud. Just before they turned off the beach exit, he reached over and took her hand. She smiled and curled her fingers around his.

Twenty minutes later they reached High Island and turned down the highway paralleling the shore. She strained to see over the dunes as they continued down the Bolivar Peninsula.

"Want to go on the ferry first then come back to the beach?" he asked.

She nodded in excitement. She'd already pinched herself twice to ensure she wasn't dreaming. They really hadn't had much time to talk about their new status, but she hoped they'd remedy that before the day was over. Then she'd have to decide at what point she dropped the bomb.

Chewing on her bottom lip, she cursed her stupidity for the thousandth time. If she'd only played it cool, she might be in this same position with Simon without the burden of being pregnant with a child he didn't know about.

No, she wouldn't regret it. Wouldn't allow herself to wish her baby's existence away. True it would be difficult to face Simon with the truth, but if things went well between them, it might not be as traumatic as she imagined.

When she looked up they were pulling into line for the ferry boarding. Gulls swarmed overhead, lighting on the dock masts beside the boat. The drove up the ramp and parked.

"Come on," he said, grabbing a bag with several pieces of bread in it. "Let's go feed the gulls."

They weaved through the cars and stood at the back of the ferry where the gulls were already hovering. As they motored away from the dock, Toni tossed up bits of bread for the hungry birds. The gulls followed across the bay the entire way, swooping and diving to catch the bread thrown their way.

When their bread was gone, Simon pulled her back against his chest, wrapping his arms around her. He rested his chin on the top of her head and looked out over the bay with her.

"Look!" she said excitedly, pointing out over the edge of the ferry. A school of dolphins surfaced, their bodies arcing through the water in graceful unison.

They continued watching as the dolphins disappeared from view. "That was fun," she said bestowing a wide smile on Simon. And it was the truth. This was shaping up to be the best day of her twenty-five years.

When the ferry docked, they climbed back into Simon's truck. "Do you want to hang out here in Galveston or get back on the ferry?"

She fastened her seat belt and thought for a moment. "Let's go back. There won't be many people on the peninsula so we'll have the beaches to ourselves."

"I like the way you think," he said with a grin.

As they returned to the line waiting for the next ferry, she wondered, not for the first time, if they were doing the right thing. She hated this subtle awkwardness between them. Almost as if neither of them truly felt at ease with the transition they were trying to make.

If things didn't work out, their friendship could very well fall by the wayside.

🚌 🚌 🚌

After dinner and a long walk on the beach, they packed the cooler back up and returned to the truck to head home. They rode in silence, Toni staring out her window at the passing landscape.

"You okay?" Simon asked glancing over at her.

She offered him a smile. "Just tired."

"I hope we didn't overdo it."

"Of course not. I had a wonderful time."

"So did I," he said after a moment.

She studied his profile as he drove, the ripple of muscles visible in his arms. She could never explain the urge that overtook her when she was around him, but she physically had to restrain herself to keep her from throwing herself in his arms. Burying her head in his broad chest and feeling his strong arms around her.

"What are you thinking?" His voice rudely brought her fantasy to an end.

She flushed. "Oh nothing." She wasn't going to admit that she really wished he would kiss her again. There had been several opportunities when they'd walked the beach hand in hand, but she had felt shy and uncertain.

"You were staring awfully hard."

She looked guiltily away, but chuckled in an attempt at dry humor. "Surely you're used to girls staring at you."

"But I'm not used to you staring at me."

Swallowing a deep gulp, she chanced a look back at him. "Does it bother you?"

"I suppose it's best to be totally honest with each other," he began. "I admit, this is a little weird for me. I honest to God thought I was losing my mind when I started looking at you as something other than a good pal. I felt guilty, confused, and a little betrayed."

"Betrayed?"

"Yeah, I mean I wasn't supposed to be looking at you like that, much less thinking the things I was thinking. But I was anyway."

Her cheeks grew warm. "Yeah well, try doing that for a few years."

"Why didn't you ever say anything?" he asked.

"Why didn't you?" she countered.

"Good point. I guess we're both hopeless," he said with a chuckle.

"Is this going to ruin things, Simon?"

He took his eyes off the highway and looked at her for a moment. "No, I don't think so. I hope it will make things even better."

His hand crept over and he loosely threaded his fingers through hers.

The rest of the ride home went by in a blur. They had light conversation about nothing in particular but their hands stayed entwined.

As they pulled into the driveway at home, Toni's brow furrowed as she saw a red Honda Accord parked beside her Jeep. "Isn't that Starla's car?" she asked, though she knew exactly whose car it was.

"Yeah," he muttered as he shut off the ignition.

Not waiting for him to open the door for her, she slid out of the truck and met him around the front. Hating the intense feeling of insecurity that gripped her, she wiped the palms of her hands on her jeans as they started for the door.

A.J. met them as they stepped inside. "Thought I heard you guys." He gestured with his thumb over his shoulder and whispered, "She's been here all afternoon. Poor Matt's been stuck entertaining her."

Toni froze as Simon moved past A.J. en route to the living room. "Why is she here?" she hissed at A.J.

He shrugged as they fell in behind Simon. "I don't know but she wasn't leaving until she talked to Simon. She's been sitting here for two hours."

"Good grief."

"There you are," Starla exclaimed when they all walked into the living room. She rose from the couch where Matt sat with a very relieved look on his face. "I had about given up on you. Where on earth have you been?"

She stopped in front of Simon and casually brushed her hand across his arm. Toni looked at her in disgust, recognizing the gesture from Mike's advice to her on how to get Simon to notice her.

"Toni and I went to the beach," Simon replied.

She laughed. "This late in the year? I suppose Toni couldn't get one of the other guys to go."

"Oh please," Toni muttered. She turned and walked back into the kitchen, unable to stomach the sight of Starla and Simon together. But then she'd never been able to before either.

"Did you need something?" Simon prompted.

Toni swung around taking interest once more in the conversation behind her.

Starla looked momentarily confused then smiled brightly. "I wanted to make sure you hadn't forgotten about tomorrow."

"Oh cripes, I had forgotten," Simon said slapping his hand to his forehead.

"Forgotten what?" Toni asked walking back over.

"I promised Starla I'd drive her to Houston tomorrow," he said in an uneasy voice.

Toni's eyes narrowed. "Is there a reason she can't drive herself? I'd say she drove over here just fine."

A.J. wrapped an arm around her waist tightening his hand. He was clearly warning her not to lose her temper, but damn it, had Simon really made a date with Starla and not told her about it?

"Oh you're so funny, Toni," Starla said, her tinkly laughter rubbing over Toni like sandpaper. "You always did have such a superb sense of humor. It's no wonder Simon likes you so much."

She paused a moment, and her eyes dropped down to the swell of Toni's stomach. "And congratulations. I never did get to offer my well wishes on your pregnancy. I'm sure being a single mom will suit you perfectly."

Toni stared at Starla's hair, picturing it wrapped around her fingers as she yanked it all out. "Why thank you, Starla. Being single suits you as well." She turned around in disgust and stalked to her room unable to stomach Starla's saccharine attitude.

What had been a perfectly good day now lay in ruins. Nothing could salvage it now. Not unless a giant anvil dropped from the sky and crushed Starla in a scene reminiscent of Wylie Coyote.

She could understand why Starla was pursuing Simon. Starla would have to be nuts not to see how badly she'd screwed up. What she didn't understand, however, was why Simon wasn't telling Starla to go fly a kite. Could he still be in love with Starla? And if he was, where did that leave her?

Quickly disrobing, she stepped into the shower and turned the water on full blast. As she washed the salt and grime from her skin, she agonized over what was transpiring in the living room. She didn't even try to pretend she didn't care.

She toweled off and hastily dressed. She refused to act like a sulky child and stay in her room in a huff. Starla would not get the satisfaction of the last word. Nor would Toni allow her to see how affected she was by her presence.

But when she returned to the living room, she found both Starla and Simon gone. She stared dumfounded for a minute then looked over at A.J. "Where's Simon?"

"He took Starla home," A.J. offered reluctantly.

"Have I entered the twilight zone?" She dropped onto the couch in exasperation. "I mean I could swear I just went out on a date with Simon. Or did I imagine that part?"

A.J. stared at her clearly having no clue what to say.

"And what's up with Miss Helpless needing Simon to take her places? Did she not drive over here?"

"I don't even know what to tell you," A.J. finally said. The look of sympathy in his eyes irritated her more. Apparently Starla still had a hold on Simon. Why else would he be jumping to do her bidding? And what was with all that gibberish he'd spouted about being attracted to her if he still had a thing for Starla?

She rubbed her head in a tired gesture. What a waste of what had been a truly spectacular day. "I'm going to bed," she muttered as she rose from the couch.

"Toni, I'm sorry," A.J. offered.

"Not nearly as sorry as Simon's going to be," she said with a twist of her lips. "I'll see you on Monday, okay? Have a good one at work tomorrow."

She went back to her room and curled up with her pregnancy book. One thing was for sure. She wasn't going to sleep until she knew what time Simon came back in.

At midnight, she heard a truck pull in and moments later the kitchen door open and close. Expecting Simon to come to her room she waited for his knock. But it never came.

Finally, she set aside her book and walked quietly to her door and peeked out. The house was dark. Evidently he had gone straight to bed.

Anger simmered within her. What kind of game was he playing? Did he honestly expect her to sit quietly on the side while he continued his thing with Starla? Why had he even asked her out if he was still interested in Starla?

She crawled back in bed, angry because her perfect day lay in tatters. Before she had gone to great lengths to avoid a confrontation of any sorts. But no longer. Simon was going to hear about it.

Chapter Eighteen

Sunday Toni left the house early. There was no way she was going to spend the day waiting around for Simon to get home from chauffeuring Starla around. She was too steamed to have a coherent conversation at any rate. Better to wait until she was a great deal calmer.

Monday she sat behind the desk at the office devising a hundred ways of telling Simon exactly what she thought about him. As if she had conjured him up by sheer will, the door opened and he strode in shortly after noon.

She looked guardedly at him as he approached the desk.

He held up his hands. "Before you start I want to apologize."

"I don't think the English language has enough words to help you," she said acidly.

His green eyes looked intently at her, his expression contrite. "At least give me a chance to explain."

She made a show of checking her watch. "You've got two minutes."

"I'm sorry Starla ruined our day. I didn't know she was coming over, and I honestly forgot I had promised to drive her to Houston."

Toni leaned forward in her chair, placing her hands on the counter. "Why exactly did you agree to it in the first place?"

"She needed someone to help her."

She stood and dug her fists into her waist. "You know what your problem is, Simon? You're too nice. I don't think you've ever said no to anyone in your life."

"Somehow I never thought that would be a negative," he said dryly.

"It is when you can't say no to a dirty, lying bitch who cheated on you." Taking a deep breath, she launched into her prepared speech. "Look, Simon. I am not going to share you with Starla or anyone else for that matter. You have a choice to make and you better make it soon because at this point in the game I can't afford to waste my time with someone who isn't in it for the long haul. If you want Starla fine. Then quit screwing with me and take her back. But if you want to see where this takes us, then I need to quit seeing Starla at my house every time I turn around."

As she finished, a slow grin spread across Simon's face. "Why don't you come around the counter so I can give you my answer up close and personal." He crooked his finger at her.

She raised an eyebrow. "It seems to me it's you who ought to be groveling. You can come here."

He laughed. "Stubborn as always. All right. I'm not too proud to beg." He sauntered around the desk and came to a stop inches away from her. Then he pulled her into his arms and cupped her cheek in one palm. "I'm truly sorry. There is nothing between me and Starla, I swear. She needs a friend right now and I was the only one she could talk to."

"You must be completely blind," she muttered.

He lowered his lips to hers and tugged gently at her bottom lip with his teeth. "Can I make it up to you over dinner?" he murmured between kisses.

She felt her anger melting under his onslaught of kisses. A slight smile curved her lips. "I could be persuaded."

"Good. I'll pick you up at five and we'll drive into Beaumont."

"What about my Jeep?"

"We'll pick it up after dinner."

He kissed her lingeringly, his fingers sliding over the curve of her jaw. "I'll see you later."

She plopped back down after he'd left and struggled to remember why she'd ever been mad at him. The man was lethal. Butterflies bubbled in her stomach and a prickly chill snuck over her as she recounted his kisses.

The rest of the afternoon crept by as she kept a vigil by the clock. The minutes ticked by with agonizing slowness. She busied herself cleaning the counters then she went back and cleaned out all the cages.

At two, she assisted Doc in a spaying and afterwards he told her to go home. She checked her watch and frowned. Simon was supposed to pick her up after work, but she was a good hour and a half early. She had more than enough time to go home and shower and then she could leave her jeep at home when they went out.

Humming to herself, she hopped into her jeep and started home. Once again, as she pulled into the drive, Starla's red Accord gleamed in the sunlight. Toni frowned and shut off her engine, debating whether she even wanted to go inside.

The memory of Simon's heated kisses brought a smile to her lips, and she clamored out of the Jeep. Simon had assured her that he wasn't interested in rekindling his relationship with Starla, and she was going to believe him.

She let herself into the kitchen and looked around. She froze when she saw Simon and Starla in the living room standing by the couch. Starla's head rested on his chest and his hand hung limply on her back.

She let her keys slide from her fingertips and hit the counter with a clatter. Simon's head jerked up, his eyes flashing in surprise. "Toni…"

"Am I interrupting anything?" she asked acidly, not moving from the bar.

Starla turned red-rimmed eyes to Toni, then looked away, refusing to meet her gaze any longer. "I have to go," she mumbled, breaking away from Simon and shuffling past Toni.

Toni stared at the door until she heard Starla's car drive away. She swiveled back to Simon who was still standing in the living room wearing a grim expression. What the hell was going on?

He looked at her, his expression bleak, then he walked over and slid an arm around her shoulders. "I'm sorry you came home to that."

"Was that you giving her the brush off?" she asked, daring to hope.

He shook his head, quickly dashing her enthusiasm. "She's sick, Toni."

She lifted an eyebrow waiting for him to expound.

"Cancer."

"Oh." Her mouth rounded in shock. "Really?"

He squeezed her shoulder and pulled her into his arms. "Yeah. Cervical cancer. Her last visit to the gynecologist was her first clue. The tests just came back positive."

Realization dawned on Toni. "Was that what the trip to Houston was about?"

He nodded and suddenly Toni felt about an inch tall. "But why didn't you just say so? Why did you let me think…"

"That I was getting back with her?" he finished.

"Yeah."

He smiled. "Maybe I wanted you to be jealous. Ever think about that?"

She elbowed him in the gut, eliciting an "oof" as he moved away from her. "Well you did a bang up job," she said, glowering at him.

"She's going to go stay with her mom in Houston so she can be close to the hospital where she'll undergo treatment," he said as he pulled Toni back to him.

"Well, I wished her gone often enough, but this isn't the way I envisioned her going," she said softly.

"I know."

With effort, Toni slipped from Simon's embrace. "Where are the guys anyway?"

"They got called in," he said with a grin.

"And you didn't?" she asked in surprise.

"Well…" he drawled out the word, making it two syllables. "I did, but I said I had something important planned."

"Such as?" she asked raising her eyebrows.

"An evening with you," he murmured.

She moved closer to him again, raising her lips to his. "I like the way you think."

He swatted her on the butt. "Go get changed so we can go get something to eat."

She grinned at him and headed for her bathroom.

Thirty minutes later, they drove into Beaumont and went into a restaurant just off the interstate. They talked casually over the meal, but Toni felt his eyes on her the entire time. Delicious chills spread down her back as his gaze caressed her. Had she been successful? Did he want her as badly as she wanted him?

She had to tell him about the baby soon. She wouldn't wait until the last minute. She wanted him to get used to the idea before she gave birth. *Face it, Toni. You want the fairy tale delivery complete with proud papa coaching you through the contractions.*

It wasn't bad as fantasies go and she desperately wanted the three of them to be a family. But first, she wanted to make damn sure Simon wanted her separate from any obligation he had to their child.

She blinked as Simon paid the check then held out a hand to help her up. He tucked her fingers into his and led her out to the truck.

"What now?" she asked, surprised at how breathless she sounded.

"We can do whatever you want, but I thought an evening with the house to ourselves might be great. We could rent some movies or watch some TV. I give a mean foot massage."

"Sounds heavenly," she murmured. But she was fixated on home and alone. She gulped nervously and slid into the truck. She remembered all too well what happened the last time they were home alone.

They drove home in silence. As they walked into the darkened house, Simon flipped on the kitchen light, leaving the living room still in the shadows. "Go have a seat. I'll fix us something to drink."

She trudged over to the couch, her feet the weight of led. Anticipation bubbled and swelled in her stomach. She was terrified.

Simon set a glass of juice on the coffee table in front of her then settled down next to her. Silence loomed over them like a heavy fog. She sipped at the juice then suddenly found it taken from her grasp.

She looked over at Simon in surprise as he removed the glass and returned it to the table. "Toni…" He paused for a long moment. "I think it best if I'm up front and very honest with you about what I'm feeling right now. I don't want you to think I'm sneaking up on you or something."

Her puzzlement growing, she gave him a blank stare, wondering at his hesitancy. But what she saw in his eyes gave her the most pause. Desire. Warm and liquid. Burning brightly in the emerald depths.

She sucked in her breath feeling curiously lightheaded. He had only looked at her like that one time before and tonight there was no way he could confuse her with Starla.

"More than anything," he began softly. "I want to make love to you, Toni. I've thought of little else in the last few weeks. You've haunted my dreams, and I've gone crazy wondering what it would be like to touch you, love you."

Her heart pounded wildly and her chest tightened almost unbearably. Only in her wildest dreams had he said such words. She didn't trust herself to speak so she did the only thing she could manage. She leaned forward and wrapped her arms around him, kissing him with all the need, desire and longing she had felt for so long.

He groaned deep in his throat and tore his lips away. "Are you sure?" he asked hoarsely.

"I'm very sure," she said softly.

He pulled her to him, tangling his hands in her hair as he took possession of her lips once more. Gently, he curled his arm underneath her legs and stood up, sweeping her into his arms. Never taking his lips from hers, he walked into her bedroom and kicked the door shut with his foot.

At the bed, he laid her on the covers and stood staring down at her, his eyes blazing with need. She swallowed as he pulled his shirt over his head, his muscles rippling with the effort.

She couldn't tear her eyes from him, his large arms, his broad chest with just a hint of hair in the hollow of his breast plate. She followed the line of hair down to his navel, resenting the waistband of his pants for preventing her gaze from dropping lower.

As if sensing her chagrin, he unbuttoned his pants and slowly unzipped them. Her breath caught in her throat as he slid his jeans down his legs. Her eyes yanked back up to meet his, and she shivered under his intense stare. There was not a single part of her that felt untouched by his penetrating gaze.

Finally, he hooked his thumbs in his underwear and pulled them down. She stared unabashedly at his erection. If she had any doubt before that he wanted her, it was now hastily removed.

The bed dipped as he slid his naked body over her fully clothed one. His skin felt warm, rugged, and decidedly masculine under her hands as she stroked her fingers up his back and over his shoulders.

"I want this to be perfect," he rasped, kissing her lips, her chin, her nose, her neck.

He slid a hand under her shirt, seeking the clasp of her bra. Soon it fell loose and he smoothed his fingers over the swell of her breast, seeking the taut nipple. She moaned as he thumbed the stiff peak. Sparks of pleasure radiated over her body in lightning speed.

He shifted over her, settling his weight on one elbow. With his free hand, he shoved impatiently at her shirt, pushing it over her head then pulling it free, bearing her breasts to his avid gaze.

Her nipples tightened unbearably as his mouth hovered temptingly over one. "Please," she whispered.

"Please what?" he murmured, blowing hot air over the tip.

She groaned. "Taste it," she pleaded.

He sucked the nipple between his teeth and laved his tongue over it. She arched spasmodically, unable to control the liquid heat that snaked through her body.

Not releasing her nipple, he reached down to shove at her pants, working them over her hips. Soon she wore only her thin panties. "You are so damn beautiful." He looked down at her as if memorizing every nuance of her body.

Then he bent and pressed a kiss to the swell of her stomach, molding it with his hands. Tears sprang to her eyes as he lavished attention on her body. How perfect this was. Nothing could make the moment any better.

Gently, his hand worked into her underwear, shoving it down and out of the way. He parted her legs, giving him easier access to the soft curls between her thighs. "I'm going to make love to you all night. I don't think I'll ever get tired of it," he whispered as he pressed his lips to hers again.

She wrapped her arms around his neck, trapping him against her. Her body squirmed, restless, hot, aching, needing. She wanted what only he could give her.

She felt flushed, sexy, alive. Like she was the only woman in the world. The only woman he would ever want. It was a heady feeling. She was lost in the electric sensations of his lovemaking.

As he moved over her, covering her with his body and nudging her legs apart with his thigh, she arched into him once again. She gripped his shoulders, her nails digging into the thick muscles as he slowly entered her. His eyes were fastened to hers, locking them together as he moved into her, making them one.

Tears glistened on her eyelashes and she tried to blink them away. He kissed them away instead as he came to a stop within her.

It was even better than before. He was making love to her. Not anyone else. He saw only her.

She locked her legs around his hips, seeking to seat him further inside her. He moaned a delicious, desperate sound. A man valiantly trying to maintain control over his raging need. She smiled, a temptress confident in her ability to drive him mad.

She began to move restlessly against him, spurring him to more action. He growled possessively and kissed her savagely, moving forward with deep, soul wrenching thrusts. But his touch was gentle, his hands touching her almost reverently as if afraid she'd shatter into a million pieces. And she felt dangerously close to doing just that.

Her release built slowly, then faster, higher and more powerful until she feared she could take no more. Then suddenly as she heard him call out her name—*her name*—she burst into flames, the explosion within her violent. She clutched desperately at him, wanting to anchor herself to him amidst the storm.

His lips, his hands, moved over her like feathers, his soothing words a balm to her heated skin. He caught her against him as he found his own release. They lay there, wrapped tightly around each other, neither moving, neither breaking the moment.

She closed her eyes, holding back the tears of exquisite pleasure. Everything she had ever dreamed of. Here in her arms. Her bed. Her heart. *I love you.*

For a moment she thought she spoke the words aloud, but Simon remained quiet against her, his hand idly stroking her hair. "I never imagined," he said in wonder.

She had. Oh yes, she had.

"And yet it all seemed so familiar," he continued on, his voice catching oddly.

She stiffened beside him, her heart pounding wildly.

He kissed her again and she relaxed, giving over to the demand of his lips. "Are you all right? Was I too rough?" he asked in concern as he cupped her stomach.

She smiled and kissed him, effectively silencing him. "If I was any righter, I'd die."

He grinned wickedly at her. "If I didn't know better, I'd say you enjoyed yourself."

She pretended to give it considerable thought. "I may have to try it a few more times before I can give you a better opinion."

He laughed. "Minx. Before tonight's over with, you'll know without a doubt."

Chapter Nineteen

Toni hummed under her breath as she puttered around the veterinarian office. She smiled a secret smile, her giddiness nearly overtaking her.

In the weeks following the night she and Simon had made love, their relationship had been nothing short of pure magic. They were together constantly, and they'd used every opportunity available to make sweet, passionate love.

Even now she melted in remembrance of his possessive kisses. He could love her. He truly could. She believed that now. She was confidant he saw her as more than little Toni Langston. She had actually gotten him to notice her.

She patted her swollen belly and grinned idiotically. At nearly six months, she'd gained a healthy bulge and she delighted in it. Simon's baby.

She frowned slightly. She had to tell him. Yeah, she'd been saying that for a long time now, but she'd have to do it soon. A flutter of uncertainty engulfed her stomach sending it into spasms of nervousness.

The right time. She'd wait for the right time.

"Mornin', Toni," Marnie sang out as she rounded the corner into the front reception area.

Toni crooked a brow and smiled as the older woman all but danced to the desk. "Mornin'. What's got you so chipper this morning?"

Marnie's eyes twinkled in delight. "Are you still thinking to move out of your house?"

"Yeah. Matt's getting married."

"I know of a place that's coming open in a week, but you'll need to act fast and put a deposit down on it."

Toni sucked in her breath. That was a lot sooner than she'd wanted, but she'd already done some preliminary looking, and the fact was, there wasn't a whole lot to rent in Cypress. Beaumont was looking more and more like it was the only option available to her, and she didn't want to move that far from everyone.

"Where is it?" she asked.

Marnie smiled again. "John's moving out of his house, and he rents it from the widow Jameson. He'll be out at the end of this week, and she plans to run an ad early next week. If you wanted though, you could run by and look at it, and if you liked it, you could talk to Ms. Jameson about renting it."

"Wait a minute," Toni said suspiciously, a broad smile beginning. "Just why is John moving out of the house he's rented for the last ten years?"

Marnie actually blushed. "Because he's moving in with me."

"Marnie you old devil!" Toni exclaimed. "How long have you two had a thing going anyway?"

"Oh awhile," she said vaguely, her blush deepening. "How about it though, you interested? I could run you by the house. John wouldn't mind you taking a look."

Toni blew out her breath. It was a good opportunity and only a mile or so from her current house. She'd be close to work still and close to the guys. "I'll run by and take a look after work if that's okay," she finally said.

"Sure. I'll call John and tell him you'll be over."

"Thanks, Marnie. I appreciate it."

As Toni bent back over the paperwork she was filing, she cursed under her breath. Simon was coming by after work and they were supposed to go eat. She'd just have to bring him along. His opinion might be worth having since sooner or later he'd have to look for a place to live as well. And maybe, just maybe... She wouldn't count her chickens before they hatched.

🚒 🚒 🚒

"You ready to go?" Simon asked as he barged through the front entrance.

Toni looked up from the desk and smiled welcomingly. "Yeah. Let me grab my purse."

As they walked out together, she turned casually to him. "Mind if we skip dinner tonight?"

He opened the door for her, and she slid into the truck. "Sure, but what's up?"

She waited until he walked around to his side and climbed in behind the wheel. "I want to go look at a house that's coming up for rent."

She held her breath, waiting for his reaction.

He turned in surprise. "But I thought you weren't going to move out until after the baby's born?"

"That was the plan, but Marnie told me about this house and it sounds perfect. And if I wait, I'll lose out."

He started the engine and backed out of the parking lot. "Okay, I'll go with you." But he was still frowning.

They drove toward their house but turned down the gravel road just before the entrance to their subdivision. A quarter mile down the dusty road, he pulled up in front of a small frame house.

The yard encompassing a half-acre at the most was quartered in with a chain length fence. Green shutters stood out against the white painted wood of the house. It looked well kept and clean even it resembled a matchbox. But then she didn't require much space for her and the baby.

John came out on the front porch as they got out and motioned them inside. Simon tucked an arm around her waist and guided her up the steps.

Once inside she looked around the small living room. Beyond, she could see the eat-in kitchen, and she moved in that direction. The space was adequate, and it had all the necessary appliances. Stove, refrigerator, microwave and dishwasher.

"There's a small laundry room off the kitchen," John said pointing to the doorway by the pantry.

As they walked toward the other end of the house, John spoke up again. "There's two bedrooms though one is about half the size of the other."

"Perfect for a baby's room," she said, beaming up at Simon. And it *was* perfect. The master bedroom was smaller than the one she currently had, but it would fit her furniture with no problem. And the second bedroom would easily fit a crib and a changing table.

The house was perfect for her, of that there was no doubt. She glanced over at Simon who had worn a perpetual frown since their arrival.

"What do you think?" she asked even though her mind was already made up.

"I don't know," he said doubtfully.

"It's perfect and you know it," she teased. "Can you tell Ms. Jameson that I'm interested?" she asked John.

"We can run over there if you like," John offered. "She lives a mile down the road."

She nodded. "Let's do it."

Simon followed her out, still frowning, but he remained silent.

Thirty minutes later, she signed a simple one-page lease and wrote a check for the deposit and one months rent. She hadn't wanted to start paying rent so soon, but it was a small price to pay if it guaranteed her a house in Cypress. And with the money she was making working part time at dispatch, she could afford it.

As she and Simon drove home, he looked over at her. "So when do you plan to move?" His voice sounded oddly strained.

She frowned, pursing her lips in thought. "Well, it doesn't make sense to pay rent and not use it, so I suppose I should move pretty quickly."

His expression darkened and she laughed. "Come on, Simon. Surely you can see the benefits." She grinned evilly at him. "Think of all that time we'll have to ourselves..." She let the thought trail off suggestively.

His eyes darkened. "You minx. I see your point."

She laughed and waggled her eyebrows at him. "Privacy has its advantages." And if she had anything to do with it, she wouldn't be alone in the house for long.

🚒 🚒 🚒

Matt and A.J. weren't thrilled with the idea, but then neither was Toni if the truth be known. When it had come down to it, she had been sad to leave the house she'd lived in for so long. But she knew it was inevitable, and it would provide her and Simon more time to work on their relationship.

Even though she had no complaints, she was still very much in the dark about how Simon felt about her. He continued to go with her to her appointments, and he seemed as excited as she was about the baby's development. They made love with an intensity that took her breath away. But he'd never really said how he felt about her.

She sighed as she packed yet another box for one of the guys to take to Simon's truck. She only had a few weeks before her self-imposed deadline for telling Simon the truth was up, and she had hoped they would have things resolved between them by then.

"You about done?" Simon asked as he stood inside the doorway to her room.

"Last one," she announced, shoving the box across the floor to him.

He hoisted it up in his arms and walked away, leaving her sitting on the floor of her empty room. She glanced around it, trying not to feel melancholy about leaving. She should be excited. For the first time since she'd gone off to college, she was striking out on her on. And frankly, she was long overdue.

She struggled to get up, stretching as she stood. A quick glance around told her she'd gotten everything.

"You sure this is what you want?" Matt asked from the door.

She looked over to see him watching her in concern. She smiled at him. "I'm sure."

He closed the distance between them and hugged her tightly. "I'm going to miss you."

She snorted even though *I'll miss you too* strained to spill from her lips. "I'm just a mile away. You aren't getting rid of me that easily."

"The door is always open here, Toni." He stared at her, his eyes serious. "You're moving out changes nothing. This is your home. You are always welcome here."

"I know," she said hugging him again. "And I won't be a stranger. I promise."

"Better not be," he said gruffly. "I'll come drag your ass out of your house kicking and screaming if I have to."

"Y'all ready?" A.J. shouted from the door.

"Be right there," she called back. "Well. That's it."

Matt threw an arm around her and guided her toward the door. "Let's go get you unpacked."

The three guys stayed to make sure Toni didn't handle any of the larger boxes. Toward dinner, Matt and A.J. made their escape but Simon stayed behind, helping Toni put away the new dishes she had bought for the kitchen.

"Want pizza? I called in an order awhile ago," she asked coming up behind him and wrapping her arms around his back.

He turned in her arms and pulled her tight against him. "Sounds good." He bent to kiss her. "Like your new house?"

"I do actually," she said with a smile. "It feels homey. And it's mine. It's a neat feeling."

"Want company tonight?" he asked innocently.

"Hmmm, sounds like a proposition to me," she said, snuggling deeper into his chest. This would be a perfect time to tell him. She faltered, finding it suddenly difficult to breathe.

She drew away and looked intently into his eyes. Eyes filled with such affection. And love? She drew in a deep breath. "Simon?"

"Yes, sweetheart?"

"There's something I need to tell you," she said in a low voice.

He looked curiously at her. "Sure, go ahead."

She opened her mouth to spill her damning secret when the doorbell rang. Nearly weak with relief at the interruption, she smiled. "Pizza's here."

🚌 🚌 🚌

Coward. Pathetic coward. She brushed her hair then threw the brush down on her dresser in disgust. She'd blown the perfect chance to tell Simon the truth. Closing her eyes, she cursed herself with vehemence. Things were only getting more complicated. Before she didn't want to tell him for fear he would commit himself to her out of obligation. Now, she feared his anger, his hatred when she was so close to gaining his love.

Feeling slightly nauseous, she made herself finish getting ready for work. Simon had left fifteen minutes ago for the station. She blushed when she imagined Matt and A.J.'s reaction to his spending the night with her.

If only she could be assured of his feelings. If he had any. No, she knew he had feelings for her. She just didn't know what *kind* of feelings.

She groaned and clenched her fists in frustration. This was eating her alive, and she couldn't take it much longer. She slipped on a light jacket and stepped out into the late Autumn morning air. It was a bit cooler than normal for this time of year, and she wondered if they were in for a colder winter. Anything colder than mild was considered frigid, she thought with a smile.

At the vet's office, she set about the morning routine as the early drop-offs for spaying and neutering flooded in. At nine when their regular patient load started to filter in, she was surprised to see Mrs. Hauffrey come in without her poodles.

"Good morning, Mrs. Hauffrey," she said politely.

"Good morning, Antonia."

"Do you need something for Fifi or Fritz?"

"Oh, I popped in to select a new collar," she said airily.

Liar. She didn't allow anything but the finest leather to touch her darlings' necks. Toni narrowed her eyes waiting for the real reason for the harridan's visit. She didn't have to wait long.

As Mrs. Hauffrey made a show of looking over the selection of collars in a display by the desk, she turned and glanced back at Toni. "I heard you moved out to the widow Jameson's house."

Toni clenched her teeth and rolled her eyes. Why her actions caused so much interest in Cypress she would never know. She was hardly worthy of an entire gossip session. "Yes, that's right," she said casually, busying herself with the charts lying on the desk.

"It's about time," the woman muttered.

"I beg your pardon?" Toni asked in disbelief.

Mrs. Hauffrey turned her full attention to Toni, smiling brightly. "I merely thought it was high time you moved out of that house. Highly inappropriate, living with *three* unmarried men. It's no wonder you ended up in your present state." Her tone was scandalized, and she puffed as she spoke.

Anger made Toni tremble, and she forgot any restraint she thought to practice. "Listen to me you, old windbag. I don't care what you or anyone else thinks about me. Those men you sneer about are my family, and if nothing else, I defend my family. If I hear so much as a word about you spreading rumors about them, I'll tell everyone what you really do when you supposedly attend Bible study in Beaumont on Tuesday nights."

Mrs. Hauffrey flushed a dark purple. She opened her mouth then closed it again, her flabby jaws flapping up and down like a sheet in the breeze. "You...how..." she sputtered off unable to complete her protest.

She turned and stalked out of the office, slamming the door shut behind her.

Toni chuckled and shook her head. She should have done it a long time ago, stood up to battleaxe, but she'd never wanted to cross the woman. Now, if the woman was smart, she'd steer clear of Toni.

After a phone call to Lonnie at dispatch to confirm her schedule for the weekend, she collected her keys and headed home. Usually she kept the same hours at dispatch as Simon did at the firehouse so they'd have the same evenings off, but tonight she was looking forward to a night alone in her new house.

As much as she had bucked the idea of moving, she now realized it was the best thing she'd ever done. She felt freer, less confined, and definitely more independent. She loved the guys, but they had smothered her for too long. And being away had given her and Simon much needed time to pursue their relationship.

The phone was ringing as she let herself in and she hurried over to answer.

"Hey, sweetheart," Simon's voice sounded over the receiver.

She smiled, unable to control her visceral reaction to his voice. "Hey. Slow night?"

"Yeah, not much going on. How was work?"

She made a face. "I told Mrs. Hauffrey off. Otherwise pretty boring."

"Whoa. What did the old bat do now?"

She related the conversation and Simon broke into laughter. They talked a few more minutes before he started to end the call. "You work in dispatch in the morning, but you have Sunday off right?"

"Yeah, same as you." He knew all this already, but she figured he was working up to something.

"You coming by to watch football on Sunday?" he asked.

She smiled, realizing what he was getting at now. The guys had likely put him up to it. "Tell Matt and A.J. I'll be there."

He laughed and hung up.

She padded out of the kitchen and into her living room. Her furniture was nothing fancy, but it was hers. She glanced around the room in pride. She'd always dreamed of having her own place. Of course, she'd always imagined having a family to go with it, and she wouldn't be renting her house. She'd own it.

With a deep sigh, she leaned back on her couch and hit the remote to turn the TV on. It could be worse. She could be completely alone.

Chapter Twenty

Toni yawned and rolled her eyes as she dispatched an ambulance to the Morrison residence. Sam Morrison dialed 911 at least once a week claiming he was smothering on the account his oxygen wasn't working. Toni thought it was more likely he was lonely and enjoyed the paramedics fussing over him.

"Slow day," Cody said with a yawn. "At this rate, we won't need Sarah to come in at noon."

Toni nodded, leaning back in her swivel chair and spinning slowly around. The scanner was even quiet, which meant a truly slow day all the way around. Dispatch kept a scanner on at all times monitoring the fire and police frequencies. Many times it allowed them to react quicker to emergencies. They could have an ambulance en route several minutes before someone called it in. In this business, a few minutes could mean the difference between life and death.

At noon Sarah came bustling in and tossed a bag at her and Cody. "I picked up lunch at Sonic," she said, as she flopped in the chair beside Toni.

"Hey thanks, Sarah," Cody said, digging into the bag immediately.

"Anything going on?" she asked as she munched on a fry.

Toni retrieved a burger from her bag and unwrapped it. "Not much. The usual."

"You want to go home early?" she asked Toni. "Since it's slow, we don't need three dispatchers.

Toni nodded. "Sure. I'll clock out after I eat."

"Take your time."

As they ate, the scanner crackled and they perked up. Toni listened intently as station two was dispatched to a fire downtown.

"That's your boys," Cody said.

"Yeah, it is. Hey did you hear what building it was?" Toni asked, listening harder to the hurried transmission.

"Thought it said the old theater," Sarah mumbled around a mouthful of burger.

"Da-mn," Cody said with a whistle. "That monstrosity's been around forever."

The scanner was quiet for a while then it came to life again as station radioed there were ten-ten, on scene. A minute later, Toni recognized the chief's voice.

"Get us some back-up. This one's a bitch."

Toni's brow lifted. Not often was there a fire major enough to warrant calling out both stations. She wondered briefly if they'd call out a crew from Beaumont.

She forgot all about leaving as she listened to the drama unfold. She chewed absently on the burger as she listened for more traffic.

Back-up arrived, and from she could discern, the fire was out of control. If it was too bad, in all likelihood, the entire block would go up where the theater was situated.

The chief crackled back over the scanner, apparently radioing for yet more back up. Toni frowned. It must be one hell of a fire. A prickle of unease skirted over her as the chief continued laying out his needs. In the background she suddenly heard shouts. Then the chief swore and yelled out presumably to someone close. "Get an ambulance here. I've got men down!"

Toni's heart lurched into her throat and she could feel every ounce of blood leaving her face. She stumbled up, the bag in her lap falling to the floor. "Toni, be careful," Sarah called as she ran for the door. Cody was already dispatching an ambulance.

She drove as fast as she felt safe to do, her pulse pounding in her temple. Several miles from downtown she saw the billowing smoke reaching toward the sky. Several streets were already blocked off, so she parked her Jeep and ran toward the building.

When she got close enough to see the theater, a scream lodged in her throat. The roof was caved in and flames shot through the opening. The fire had already spread to the bank two doors down and looked as if it would soon consume the clothing boutique on the end.

An ambulance screamed up, but her eyes were riveted to the two firemen being carried out of the burning building. Her mouth went dry even as she launched herself forward, shoving by the crowd of bystanders.

As she got to the area cordoned off by the fire crew, she ducked underneath the tape.

"Whoa there, Toni." Hands grabbed her, preventing her progress. "Honey, don't go over there."

She realized it was Mike. Tears sprang to her eyes. "It's one of them isn't it?" she whispered.

His eyes softened, regret filling his face.

She jerked away from him and ran to where the ambulance crew surrounded the men on the ground. "Oh dear God," she choked out. It wasn't *one* of them. It was Matt and Simon. Where was A.J.? She raised her head, looking frantically around for sign of him.

"Toni, you shouldn't be here," the chief said firmly, trying to steer her away.

"Don't!" she said, hardly recognizing the sob in her voice. She yanked her arm free. "Where's A.J.?" she demanded.

"He's fine," the chief said reassuringly. "Just being treated for smoke inhalation. There he is now."

A.J. must have seen her because he was bearing down on her through the crowd of people. He caught her in his arms, shielding her from her view of Simon and Matt. "They'll be okay," he said in a hoarse voice.

She gripped him tightly, nearly faint with relief. When she hadn't seen him she'd assumed the worst. But now she had to find out how Simon and Matt were. "Don't protect me, A.J.," she said fiercely. "I want to know how they are."

She shoved closer, trying to see amidst the people swarming everywhere. Her heart twisted as she saw Simon's soot covered face. His eyes were closed.

An oxygen mask was crammed over his nose and mouth after the C-collar was secure.

A paramedic looked up and saw Toni standing there. He grimaced. "Want to ride?" he asked as they loaded Simon up on the stretcher.

"A.J., can you ride with Matt?" she asked.

"Go on, babe. I'll catch you at the hospital."

She clamored into the back of the ambulance with the assistance of another fireman. They slammed the doors shut and the ambulance lurched forward.

"Sit there and buckle up," the paramedic said, gesturing toward the jump seat.

"Will he be all right?" she asked fearfully.

"Yeah, I think so. His vitals are stable. He's damn lucky."

She breathed a heavy sigh of relief, tears swelling in her eyes. "And Matt?" she prompted.

"I don't know. The other medic took him."

She chewed her knuckles as she watched the paramedic start dual IVs. Why wasn't Simon conscious? Even she knew a prolonged loss of consciousness wasn't good.

The medic pushed Simon's eyelids open and shone a penlight into the pupils. As if feeling Toni's anxious stare, he looked up at her. "I don't see any obvious sign of head injury. His pupils are equal and reactive."

He turned away from her and picked up the radio to call report to the hospital. Toni reached forward and placed a hand on Simon's forehead. She wiped some of the soot away with her fingers, willing him to open his eyes. She couldn't lose him. No. She *wouldn't* lose him. She loved this man more than life itself.

She caught herself as the ambulance came to an abrupt halt and the back doors flew open. The ER staff assisted the paramedic as they pulled the stretched out. The paramedic reached back to help Toni down before hurrying in behind the stretcher that was wheeling away.

Toni was left behind as they shoved the stretcher through the swinging doors. She stood in shock, her fingers to her lips. Behind her, more commotion ensued as Matt was wheeled in, A.J. striding in beside him.

She rushed to the stretcher, elated to see Matt was conscious.

"Toni, what the hell are you doing here?" he demanded.

She went weak with relief, donning a crooked smile. "Thank God you're okay, Matt."

He reached up to touch her cheek. "I'm fine, just a little banged up. Do me a favor and call Steph so she won't worry."

They wheeled him away as she nodded her agreement. Strong hands gripped her shoulders, squeezing comfortingly. "How was Simon?" A.J. asked.

She turned and buried her face in his chest. "He wasn't conscious, A.J. I don't know how he is." She fought to keep desperation from her voice, but she failed miserably. "I can't lose him. I can't."

"You're not going to lose him, Toni." He rubbed her back then led her over to a row of seats by the window. "You sit. I'll go call Stephanie."

He walked stiffly off, leaving dirty footprints on the polished floor. He still wore his fire gear, layers of soot and ash clinging to him like a second skin.

She closed her eyes, not wanting to think how close she had come to losing the people most important to her. What would she do without all of them?

A.J. returned in a minute and slid into the seat beside Toni. She reached over and took his hand, gripping it tightly. "Are you okay, A.J.?"

He smiled even as he coughed. "I'm fine, really. I was almost out when the roof collapsed. Matt and Simon were behind me." His eyes flashed in pain. "I should have been with them."

She cupped his cheek in her palm. "I'm very glad you weren't hurt. My heart couldn't take all three of you in the hospital."

He caught her hand and squeezed. "I'm sorry. It must have been quite a shock. I assume you heard it over the scanner."

She nodded. "Is Stephanie coming?"

"Yeah, she freaked. I told her not to kill herself getting here, that Matt was awake."

A few minutes later, a nurse came out and looked over at them. "Are you Toni and A.J.?"

They were on their feet immediately.

The nurse gestured them back. "Matt wants to see you both."

Toni rushed into the small exam room and immediately fell on Matt, hugging him fiercely. He winced and gently pushed at her. "Let me breathe, sis. If you don't let up, I'll have to put the O2 back on."

She let him go and stood back up beside A.J.

"You okay, man?" A.J. asked, relief flaring in his eyes. He'd been as worried as her she realized now, but he'd hidden it well.

"Yeah, I'm fine. Doc says I have a few bruised ribs, but otherwise, I'm right as rain."

Toni squeezed his hand tightly, unable to speak around the knot in her throat.

"Hey, how's Simon?" Matt asked, worry evident in his voice.

"I don't know yet," she said quietly. "They haven't let me see him."

"Don't worry," he said, squeezing her hand in return. "He'll be fine I'm sure."

"Steph's on her way," A.J. spoke up.

Matt groaned. "She may never let me up."

"You got that right," Stephanie announced from the door.

Toni turned to see her rush forward, panic, relief, anguish etched in her face. "I'll see you later on," she told Matt as she stepped away from the bed.

A.J. walked out with her, leaving Matt and Stephanie alone.

"I'm going to ask about Simon," she announced. "I can't take it anymore."

She flagged down a nurse in the hall who went to inquire about Simon. In a moment she returned. "You can go in and see him. He's awake now."

Toni ran to the room, her heart pounding in her chest. At the doorway, she stopped and stared, drinking in his appearance. He was propped against a pillow, his large body incongruous with the small bed. His clothing had been stripped, a sheet pulled up to his mid-drift. Some of the soot had been cleaned from his face, but streaks still shone on his tanned skin.

With a cry, she launched herself at him. He caught her against him as she reached the bed. He enfolded her in his arms as she buried her face against his chest. Her tears fell rapidly now, wetting his skin.

"Hey," he said softly, trying to pick her head up. "I'm okay. Don't cry, sweetheart."

She raised her head, tears blurring her vision. She ran her hands over his face, reassuring herself he was alive. "I was so scared," she said in anguish. "Oh God, Simon. I almost lost you."

"I'm not going anywhere, baby. Don't cry. It's not good for the baby for you to be so upset." His hands soothed away the tears, and he pulled her face to his, capturing her lips in an emotional kiss.

"I love you, Simon," she declared, not caring what he thought of her revelation. "I've loved you forever. And when I think about what could have happened today, it nearly kills me." She sobbed openly, wrapping her arms around him and squeezing him tightly against her.

She ran her fingers through his hair then over his face, touching him, reassuring herself he was whole. She leaned her forehead against his, trying desperately to compose herself. They closed their eyes, and he wrapped his arms around her waist, running his hands over her back.

A noise from the door had Toni jerking away. "Sorry to interrupt," A.J. said with a grin. "I wanted to see how you were doing, Simon."

He walked further into the room, and Simon situated Toni beside him on the bed, tucking her under his arm.

"I'm doing okay," Simon replied. "How are you? How's Matt?"

"I'm fine. Just a bit of smoke inhalation. Matt's got a few busted ribs, but he's all right, and Steph's fussing over him."

Simon grinned. Toni turned to him. "What did the doctor say about you?"

"He cleared my spine. Said I got a knock on the head, probably from falling debris, but nothing serious. He said my lungs will feel like crap for a day or two from all the smoke, but all in all he said I was lucky."

She shivered, unable to contemplate the alternative. Her fright, the unspeakable agony she'd endured as she waited to hear Matt and Simon's condition was rapidly catching up to her. She shook almost uncontrollably. Simon's arms tightened around her, and he and A.J. exchanged worried glances.

"I need to go to the bathroom," she said shakily. Her bladder felt near to bursting, and she desperately needed to compose herself.

"Want me to go with you?" A.J. asked, looking doubtfully at her.

She smiled. "I'm fine. Besides, I don't think it's a good idea if you go into the ladies' bathroom."

"If you aren't back in five minutes, I'm sending him in after you," Simon said firmly.

She struggled down from the bed and tested her shaky legs. She wavered on the way to the door, feeling a hysterical urge to laugh.

A.J.'s hand gripped her elbow as she passed him. "I'm fine," she said brightly. "Really. I just need to use the bathroom. I'll be fine."

Simon watched her go, a combination of worry and awe occupying his thoughts. "She loves me," he said softly when she disappeared from view.

A.J. snorted. "You've only just now figured that out? Where've you been, dude? I think you suffered more than a knock on the head."

"No, she told me. She said it. She loves me." He couldn't keep the incredulity from his voice. It seemed monumental. She loved him.

A.J. laughed. "You've got it bad. That little brunette has you twisted in knots." His expression grew serious. "You scared the hell out of her today. You scared us all," he amended.

"I hope she wasn't too upset," Simon said. Her tear-filled eyes were more than he could bear.

A.J. rolled his eyes. "Let's see. The guy she loves is carried out of a burning building and rushed to a hospital. No. I don't think she was too upset." He paused and looked intently back at Simon. Simon realized then that A.J. had been just as worried.

"I'm okay, man. I swear it."

"You took a few years off my life when I had to go back in after you," A.J. admitted. "All I could think about was what if I couldn't get you and Matt out. I sure as hell wasn't going to leave you in there."

"Thanks, A.J." Simon reached out and grasped A.J.'s arm. A.J. hesitated then he wrapped his beefy arms around Simon, nearly squeezing the breath out of him. "You'd do the same for me," he said gruffly.

"Damn straight," Simon said with a nod. He frowned. "Maybe you should go look for Toni. She didn't look too good when she left."

"Don't mess this up, Simon," A.J. said quietly. "You know how she feels now. Don't wait too long to do something about it."

Chapter Twenty-One

She loved him. It was only beginning to sink in on him. The enormity of what she had said. He remembered all too clearly her earnest declaration, her heart in her eyes. It had humbled in a way nothing else ever had.

Simon sat back on the couch, watching Toni and A.J. haphazardly decorate the Christmas tree. Since he and Matt had been released two days ago, Toni had all but moved back in to fuss over them. He liked having her back around. He'd missed her even though he had spent so much time at her new place. And in her bed.

She loved him. He marveled at how such a sentiment made him feel. Starla had professed love for him, but it hadn't made him *feel* like this.

He watched her every movement, how her shirt snuck up over her gently rounded abdomen when she reached to put an ornament high on the tree. A fierce wave of possessiveness stole over him with lightning speed.

She was his. Or was she? She loved him, but what about the father of her baby? Months after her shocking announcement, she remained as tight-lipped as ever about the father's identity. Had he hurt her that bad? Or had she screwed up that bad?

His mind swirled with questions. Questions he needed answers to if he and Toni were going to have a future. He grinned as she swatted A.J. and scolded him for putting the angel on crooked. Yes, they had to have a future. He couldn't imagine one—his future—without her. She'd become as integral to him as breathing. He loved her.

His chest tightened. God, yes, he loved her. Hadn't he always? He frowned. Thinking back, there wasn't a time he hadn't felt deeply for her. Even when he dated other women, he'd always imagined he wanted someone like Toni. And when Starla betrayed him, all he could think was that Toni would never have let him down like that.

Was he ready to put it all on the line again like he'd almost done with Starla? The answer was a resounding yes. Toni was very different than Starla. Toni loved him. Toni was the kind of girl every guy dreamed of having.

A slow smile worked the corners of his mouth upward. Soon his jaw ached from the wide smile he wore. Yeah, she was his future. He loved her, and he'd love her child. Their child. His mind went to work, pondering when the best time would be to put into action his plan.

Toni glanced over at Simon to see his face split into a silly grin. She paused hanging ornaments and arched her brow. "Are we that amusing?" she asked.

His face grew serious. "You're gorgeous. I love watching you."

She flushed, feeling heat creep over her skin. He'd never been very demonstrative in front of Matt and A.J., though both knew a great deal about their relationship, including keeping quiet about the number of nights Simon spent at Toni's house.

A.J. rolled his eyes. "Could you two cut it out? I just ate."

"Why don't you get back to hanging ornaments?" she said, scowling at him. "A woman can never hear she's gorgeous too many times. Especially when said woman is as big as a house." She looked ruefully down at her full belly.

"Come here," Simon said crooking his finger at her. His eyes were dark, his expression almost angry.

She walked over to where he sat on the couch, his feet propped up on the coffee table. He caught her around the waist and pulled her down to him. "You're beautiful," he murmured. "Belly and all." He brushed his lips across hers, nibbling at the corners of her mouth.

She sighed, allowing herself to get lost in his kiss. It was easy to forget everything in his arms. Revel in the fact he was home and okay. But now she was faced with reality. She had to tell him the truth, and she had to do it now. As soon as she got the opportunity and not a minute later.

He pulled her onto his lap and held her against his chest. She smiled and cuddled further into his embrace. "I guess I get to finish this monstrosity by myself," A.J. grumbled.

"You're a doll, A.J.," she said, grinning at him.

"Yeah, yeah. A regular Cabbage Patch."

"I need to check on Matt," she said, reluctantly pulling away from Simon. "He's been asleep for awhile, and I want to make sure he doesn't need more pain medication."

"He's fine," Simon said, pulling her back into his arms. "I like you just where you're at."

"What do you say we have dinner at my place tomorrow night?" she asked lightly. Her stomach turned viciously. She'd use the opportunity to tell him her awful secret. She wiped her hands on her jeans, wanting to rid herself of the clammy feeling.

"I think that's the best idea you've had all day," he said softly. "I think there's a few things we need to talk about."

Her heart sped up. What did he mean? He couldn't possibly know. Stop. Of course he couldn't know. But he would tomorrow night because she wasn't going to put it off another day. She only prayed when he found out the truth he wouldn't hate her.

🚒 🚒 🚒

Simon got up early the next morning, a sense of purpose marking his movements. He still ached a bit from the accident, but he'd been damn lucky he hadn't been laid up for a long time. Or worse, been unable to return to work. Even Matt would be returning to the job.

"Where's the fire?" A.J. asked, as Simon hurriedly ate a bowl of cereal. He sauntered in and sat next to Simon at the bar.

"Bad joke," Simon said sourly.

A.J. laughed. "I guess so. So what's up? Aren't you supposed to be resting?"

Simon took a deep breath. "I need to go shopping for a ring. I plan to ask Toni to marry me tonight."

A.J.'s face split into a wide grin. "Hot damn. It's about time."

He grinned crookedly. "Now let's hope she says yes."

A.J. looked at him like he'd started singing opera or something. "No way she'll say no. That girl has it bad for you."

Simon smiled. "Yeah well, I have it just as bad for her. I love her," he added.

"That's great, man. Congratulations. Looks like both you and Matt will be taking the leap."

Simon searched A.J.'s face for any sign of animosity. "So how do you feel about that?"

A.J. looked surprised for a moment. "I'm thrilled. Especially for you and Toni. She's a great girl. I was ready to kick your ass if you didn't get a clue real soon."

"Yeah, well, I can't believe it took me this long to realize it," he said ruefully.

"What are you going to do about...uh, you know, the baby?" A.J. asked.

"Tell me something, A.J. And level with me. Has she ever told you who the father is?"

"No, she hasn't. I've asked her enough times, but the subject has been off limits."

Simon drew in his breath. He hoped it wasn't a case of Toni being in love with the asshole who got her pregnant. For all he knew she could have told the jerk she was pregnant, and he could have blown her off. "I can't tell you how many times I've wished it was my baby she was carrying," he said quietly. "It would certainly make things easier. And if I'm honest, I'm jealous as hell at the idea of another guy being with her."

"I can understand that," A.J. replied empathetically. "Does it bother you a lot that she's pregnant with someone else's baby? I mean will it affect how you feel about the baby?"

"It doesn't matter to me, but we're going to have to talk about it," he said. "I need to know this guy isn't going to be turning up in a few months."

"Well good luck, dude. And congratulations. I don't imagine she'll turn you down." He got up and slapped Simon on the back. "I'm gonna go check in on Matt. Let me know how it goes."

"Thanks, A.J."

Simon collected his keys and headed for his truck. He had a lot to do before going over to Toni's tonight.

🚒 🚒 🚒

At six, Simon pulled into Toni's driveway and parked his truck. He felt for the ring in his pocket before getting out and heading to her front door.

When she opened it, he pulled her into his arms, loving the way she felt, the way she fit so perfectly under his chin. He tilted her head up and kissed her delectable full lips. She tasted sensational. He could spend the rest of the evening sampling her mouth.

She shivered against him, and he quickly shut the door behind him. "Sorry," he apologized. "Didn't mean to keep you standing in the doorway."

She smiled up at him, nearly taking his breath away. He longed to taste her dimples. Christ. He was obsessed with tasting all over her tonight.

"It's cold tonight."

He nodded and shrugged out of his coat, hanging it by the door. "Yeah, weird huh. Weather said a real doozy of a cold front was heading through in the next few days."

She shook her head as they walked into the living room. "Two days ago it was in the seventies."

"Anything you want me to help you with?" he asked, as they made their way into the kitchen. He sniffed the air appreciatively. "Smells good."

She smiled again, and his eyes roved over her glowing skin. Pregnancy definitely agreed with her. Her skin was positively lickable. It was a tempting idea to keep her pregnant all the time once they were married. He smiled at his arrogance. He was sure she wasn't going to refuse.

He put his arms around her while she stirred at the stove. Quite simply he couldn't keep his hands off her. He loved the feel of her in his arms. He'd never considered himself to be an overly possessive person, but what he felt around Toni defied reasonable explanation. He wanted to spend the rest of his life taking care of her. Loving her, laughing with her, making wicked love to her.

She turned in his arms and kissed him lightly on the lips. "You can set the table if you like. Supper will be done in a few minutes."

"You mean you aren't on the menu?" he murmured as he kissed his way down her neck.

She laughed, though it sounded forced. Her eyes skirted away from him briefly. "Is something wrong?" he asked.

"No, not at all," she said brightly. "Go on and set the table. I need to take the rolls out of the oven."

He collected two plates from the cabinet then retrieved forks and knives from the dishwasher. After he set them on the table, he poured two glasses of tea. "Here, let me," he said, taking the heavy pot from her. He carried it over to the table while she collected the colander to drain the pasta.

They settled down at the table and served up plates of spaghetti. He barely managed to suppress a smile at the thought of presenting the ring to her. After supper, he told himself. They could cozy up in the living room, and he'd pour out his heart to her.

As he helped her clear away the dishes, he sensed she was on edge. "Go on in the living room. I'll finish up in here," he said, rubbing her shoulders.

As he watched her go, he experienced a moment of unease. Why was she so uptight? It could be a pregnancy thing. Maybe her back hurt. Whatever the case, he hoped his proposal provided a quick fix.

Toni escaped to the living room nearly in full-blown panic. The evening had been perfect. Just perfect. Too perfect. And now she was going to ruin it by giving Simon the shock of his life.

She paced back and forth as she waited for him to make an appearance. Her stomach was in knots, and she feared she was going to have to make a dash to the bathroom to puke. God, why had she ever gotten herself into this mess? Why hadn't she confessed what had happened the very next morning?

She looked up in dismay when Simon walked into the living room, a gentle smile on his face. He walked up to her, his eyes glowing warmly. She nearly melted in a puddle at his feet when he took her in his arms and kissed her lingeringly. "Supper was fantastic," he murmured. "But now that it's over, there's something I want to talk to you about."

She gave a nervous laugh. "How funny because there's something I wanted to talk to you about too."

"Me first," he said.

She gulped and nodded. He led her over to the couch and sat down beside her. He collected her hand in his and pressed a kiss to her upturned palm. "I love you, Toni."

His blunt statement made her jaw drop. Tears gathered in the corners of her eyes. How she'd dreamed of him saying those words. And here he was, holding her gently, gazing at her in adoration and saying those three little words. And she felt like the biggest heel in the world.

"I think I've loved you for a very long time," he admitted. "But it took you trying to get my notice that made me examine my feelings for you. And then at the hospital when you told me you loved me, it made me realize how *lucky* I was. And how stupid I'd been not to have made you mine a long time ago."

A single tear slipped down her cheek, and he thumbed it gently out of the way. She wanted to squeeze her eyes shut, look away, anywhere but into his eyes. If someone had laid a cement block on her chest, she couldn't feel any more weighted down. She didn't deserve him.

"But I want to rectify that Toni. I want to take things to the next level. But before we do that, there are things we need to talk about. Things we need to get out in the open."

She looked at him with all the weight of her guilt bearing down on her harder all the time. Soon she'd be unable to breathe at all. She opened her mouth to speak, but all words fled her like a speeding bullet.

"Toni," he prompted gently. "I need to know about the father of your baby."

Chapter Twenty-Two

She felt very close to fainting. Simon must have registered the shock she was feeling because he leaned forward, framing her face in his hands. "Don't be afraid, sweetheart. We need to talk about this though. Get it off your chest. We need to determine how this affects our future. I'm not going anywhere. But we need to get this out in the open."

She closed her eyes, tears slipping down her cheeks. After everything it had come down to this. The man she was desperately in love with was sitting in front of her prepared to propose, and she was set to drive a knife in his back.

"I don't even know how to tell you this," she said choking back a sob.

"Honey, you need to calm down. I had no idea this would upset you so badly. This isn't how I pictured the evening going at all." He paused a moment and ran a hand through his hair. "Would you prefer we talk about it another time?"

"No! I mean…no. I had planned to tell you tonight anyway. It's why I invited you over." She sucked in her breath until it made her feel light-headed.

She was too close to him. She stood up, his hands dropping from her arms. A few steps away from the couch, she turned around, daring to look at him. His eyes were alight in confusion and intense curiosity.

"Do you remember the night you and Starla broke up?" she asked.

Surprise registered on his face. "Yes, of course."

"You came home upset. You'd had something to drink. Then I sat up with you while you got drunker."

"Yeah, I remember," he said, looking away. "Not the proudest moment of my life."

"Nor was it mine," she whispered. "We had sex that night."

She watched disbelief then shock creep across his face. "Are you saying...are you saying I put a move on you?" he asked hoarsely. "Oh my God," he whispered before she could answer. "Are you saying I took advantage of you when I was drunk?" Self-loathing clouded his voice, his anguish her undoing.

"No!" she sobbed out. "That isn't the way it happened. Simon, I wanted it to happen. I encouraged you. I kissed you and it went from there. I knew you had no idea what you were doing. I had this fantasy built up in my mind. I knew exactly what I was doing, and I seduced you."

He sat shaking his head in utter disbelief. Then he paled, all the color fading from his face in a rush. "The baby. It's *mine*?"

She shook her head miserably.

He stared at her in horror. "And you never told me? You let me go all these months and the baby is mine?"

Again she nodded, unable to speak. Her hands shook violently as she awaited the explosion.

"How *could* you?" Revulsion twisted his face. "Jesus. I can't believe it. Not you, Toni. I trusted you. Tell me you didn't do this. Didn't keep something so important from me."

She pressed her knuckles to her mouth unable to hold back the sobs any longer.

He waved his hand in front of him. "This game. This charade you put on. The flirting. The effort to make me jealous. Was it real? Or did you just fear you wouldn't have a father for you baby? Damn it, Toni. Why didn't you tell me?" His voice rose and he stood up, his fists clenched by his side. "Has this all been just one gigantic joke to you? Have you been laughing at me behind my back all this time? You despise Starla so much, but you're no better than her. My God, I *trusted* you."

The pain in his face, his eyes, his voice sliced through her like the sharpest blade. "Simon, it wasn't like that," she began.

"Then tell me, Toni. What was it like?" His bitter words rang across the room.

"I was afraid," she admitted. "Afraid of messing things up between us, afraid of messing things up between all four of us."

"I see, and keeping the fact that you slept with me, much less that you were pregnant with my child from me isn't messing things up?"

"It was wrong," she said softly.

"It wasn't just wrong, Toni. It was despicable. I honestly never thought you were capable of such deceit. I am certainly not proud of the fact I had sex with a woman and apparently can't remember it, much less that it was with my supposed best friend, but what you did was unthinkable. You should have told me. *Immediately*. There was no reason for you to have gone through any of it alone."

She turned away, her head aching from the tears she'd cried. She heard him walk across the floor, and she whirled around in time to see him walk out the front door. "Simon!" she called out, racing to the door. "Don't go. We need to talk."

He paused on the porch and slowly turned around to face her. What she saw in his eyes made her flinch. "I don't have anything to say to you, Toni."

She froze at the anger, the hatred in his voice. As he walked away, her heart shattered into a million pieces. She watched in agony as he drove off. Out of her life.

She stood there for a long time, numb to the cold. Numb to anything but the searing pain in her chest. Then she slowly turned and walked back into the house.

🚒 🚒 🚒

Simon pounded the steering wheel in rage. Tears nearly blinded his vision as he tore down the road. How could she have betrayed him like this? Never would he have put her in the same category as Starla. But to allow him to go to the doctor's visits with her, pursue a relationship with him, all the while pregnant with his child. *His child.*

He'd never felt so angry, so utterly pissed off in his life. Her deception was unthinkable. And it made him sick to his stomach that the woman he loved and wanted to spend the rest of his life with had lied to him from the beginning of their relationship.

He pulled into the driveway of his house and slammed out of the truck. His mood was black, and he'd never hurt as much as he did at this moment. His fingers curled around the box the engagement ring was nestled in. In an angry motion he sent it flying across the kitchen as he stepped in the door.

"Whoa, dude." A.J. stepped back as Simon made his entrance.

Simon cursed under his breath. No one was supposed to be home. From the living room, he heard Matt get up and join them in the kitchen. Was the whole bloody world staying home tonight?

"What's going on?" Matt asked with a frown as he leaned against the bar.

"I don't want to talk about it," he managed to grit out. He closed his eyes, vowing not to shed a single tear in front of the guys.

"I take it the evening didn't go as planned," A.J. said quietly.

"Observant aren't you," Simon snarled.

"What the hell are you two talking about?" Matt demanded. "As usual, I'm in the dark."

"She say no?" A.J. pressed.

"I didn't ask," he replied bitterly.

"Why do I get the feeling you two are talking about Toni," Matt said in a dangerous tone. "One of you better spill it."

Anger swelled and overflowed, exploding out of him before he could call it back. "Your sister is a lying, conniving bitch."

Matt's jaw dropped open then a dangerous glint surfaced in his eyes. He advanced on Simon, his expression murderous. A.J. didn't look any happier, but at least he was keeping his distance.

"You better have a damn good reason for calling my sister names," Matt said softly.

"Who's the father?" A.J. asked, correctly perceiving the source of his anger.

"I am," he spat out, thumbing himself in the chest.

"What the…" Matt began.

"Say what?" A.J. sputtered. "Say that again?"

In sparse words, he related the events of the night he and Starla had broken up. By the time he finished, A.J.'s mouth was on the floor, and Matt had sunk down on a barstool.

"What was she thinking?" Matt asked in disbelief. "That's about the most hare-brained thing she's ever managed."

A.J. remained silent as he stared between the two of them. Simon threw open the fridge and popped a beer. He took a long swig then looked at it in disgust. This is what got him into this situation in the first place.

He glanced back over at A.J. who stood staring at him. "Did you break up with her?" he asked.

"Break up with her? Breaking up implies a relationship of sorts," Simon said with a snort. "Apparently I was under the mistaken impression we had a relationship. I couldn't have been more wrong."

Matt shook his head. "I can't believe she would do something like that."

"I don't think it's fair to gang up on her," A.J. said quietly. "We've only heard Simon's side of things."

Simon whirled and pinned A.J. with the full force of his glare. "You think I would lie about something like this?"

"Not at all," he returned mildly. "But we haven't heard Toni's reasons for doing what she did. I for one don't think it's any of my business, therefore, I refuse to pass judgment."

"It was a stupid thing to do," Matt insisted.

"I don't think stupid covers it," Simon muttered.

"Look, I know you're blown away by this," A.J. began. "Who wouldn't be? But my advice is to sit on it a few days. Don't make any decisions you'll regret later. I refuse to think Toni did this maliciously."

"You're entitled to your opinion, A.J. But tell me this. Why the hell didn't she tell me when she found out she was pregnant? I can almost understand why she didn't say anything about us going to bed together. It's certainly not something I'm proud of. But when she found out she was pregnant she should have told me immediately. I had the *right* to know."

"Just don't do anything you'll regret," A.J. repeated as he headed toward his room.

"Sorry, man," Matt offered.

"Yeah, me too." He turned and retreated to his room, shutting the door on his disillusionment.

🚌 🚌 🚌

The wind blew cold off the water, biting through the thin shirt she wore. Toni sat on the sand, her knees hugged to her swollen belly. The water rolled closer as the tide swept in, but still she didn't move, her gaze fixed on a distant point on the horizon.

She'd driven aimlessly until she found herself heading down the interstate toward the coast. She and Simon had sat on this very beach watching the sun go down on their first date. It seemed a lifetime ago.

Tears she didn't think she had left slipped down her cheek, burning a single trail of despair. By now Matt and A.J. would know what had happened. Matt would be angry that she had acted so rashly. She had no idea what A.J. would think. He'd probably be hurt that she hadn't confided in him. But most of all, Simon was lost to her. She would never get over that.

And she had nobody to blame but herself.

How could she face any of them? Her heart ached. Heavy and hurting. How could she pick up and go on? No matter that her relationship with Simon was over, when he calmed down, he would want to be a part of their baby's life. The worst kind of torture would be being tied to him through their child, having to be near him and knowing he hated her.

She laid her head forward on her arms and let deep welling sobs escape her. She sounded hoarse and raw, but she didn't care. She'd not only lost the man she loved, she'd lost her best friend as well.

She stayed there through the night, staring out over the great expanse of water. The tide came in. The tide went out. Before long, the sun started to peep up, bathing the beach in soft light. And still she sat, huddled on the sand with only her regrets to keep her warm.

She knew she needed to get to a phone. Call Doc and tell him she wouldn't be in, but she couldn't bring herself to move. With a frown, she checked her watch, her bleary eyes registering that it was past seven.

Sighing, she stretched her cramped legs and struggled to get up. Whatever her difficulties, she owed it to Doc to at least give him a call. He'd worry if she didn't show up.

She drove further down the peninsula and stopped at a gas station to use a payphone. She left word with Marnie, not bothering to expound on her reason for missing work. As she slid back into her Jeep, she gripped the steering wheel, gritting her teeth to keep the tears at bay. Her head felt like a cabbage, and her eyes were swollen and raw.

No idea where to go, but she wasn't going home. Not yet. She didn't want to be anywhere near Simon. The disgust in his eyes had nearly killed her. Never had she imagined him looking at her like that.

She finally turned her Jeep toward the ferry, arriving fifteen minutes later. She got right on and sat in her car while the ferry crossed the bay. It was cold. It was miserable. The weather was a perfect match for her mood.

Once in Galveston, she stopped at a fast food joint and grabbed breakfast, though her stomach rebelled at the idea of food. She then parked along the seawall and sat in her Jeep watching the waves roll in.

She didn't need to be a rocket scientist to figure out she'd screwed up royally.

Chapter Twenty-Three

A.J. replaced the phone on the base and looked over at Matt. "I don't like it. She's still not there."

"She's probably just not answering her phone," Matt suggested.

"No, I drove by there this morning. Her Jeep wasn't there and she's not at work."

"Well, she screwed up, man. I mean she's my sister, and I love her, but she's screwed the pooch this time. Maybe she decided to hide out for a few days."

A.J. frowned. "Dude, she's pregnant and probably upset as hell. You saw Simon. I doubt he just quietly walked away. Pull your head out of your ass. You and I have no reason to be angry with her."

Matt's eyes flashed. "She could have ruined our friendship. Hell, she probably already has. I doubt seriously Simon's going to want to hang around much anymore if she's here."

"You are messed up," A.J. said quietly. "She's your sister, and she's my friend. Simon isn't blameless in all this. I'm worried about her even if you aren't."

"I don't think there's anything to worry about," Matt said. "Give her time to cool off. She's always been like that."

A.J. shook his head but didn't respond. He had a bad feeling about this, and he'd feel a hell of a lot better if he knew where Toni was.

By noon, Toni was either too tired to know better or she'd decided she stood to lose nothing by calling Simon. Maybe today he was calmer. Maybe they could talk things out. And maybe she was nuts.

On the way back from Galveston, she stopped by the same gas station as before and nervously picked up the phone to call the house. She stood in the booth holding the receiver, her fingers poised over the numbers. Coward. This is what got you into this mess to begin with.

Before she lost her nerve, she punched in the phone number and waited with growing dread for someone to pick up. She shook from the cold, her face like a block of ice from the wind blowing over her tear stained cheeks. To her extreme relief, Simon picked up on the second ring.

"Simon?" she asked tentatively.

"What do you want," he cut in before she could say anything further.

"I—I thought we could talk. Can we meet somewhere?" Her voice shook, and her grip tightened on the receiver in an attempt to bolster her waning courage.

"We have nothing to talk about."

He hung up before she could respond, leaving her standing with the phone still to her ear. Slowly she cradled it back and stepped from the booth. Something in side her broke. She could literally feel it snap. Her mind seemed to break apart from her body and float free above her. She ceased to feel the biting wind, even as it began to spit tiny ice crystals.

Numbly, she returned to her Jeep, unsure of exactly what to do next. The thought of driving an hour and fifteen minutes home was unbearable. She wasn't sure she was in any shape to drive anyway. She hadn't slept in twenty-four hours.

Making a quick decision, she spun her Jeep around and drove to the only hotel on the peninsula, a run down cheap sleep a few miles from the ferry.

After securing her key, she let herself into the dark room, not bothering to turn on the lights or open the curtains. She crawled into the threadbare bed and cried herself to sleep.

🚲 🚲 🚲

"I still don't like this," A.J. said grimly as the guys stowed their gear in their lockers.

"What don't you like?" Simon asked, though he pretended interest. All his thoughts centered on a petite, brown haired, brown-eyed temptress. His emotions had calmed from deep anger to extreme disappointment and sadness. He loved her. There was no doubt about that. But what she had done had stunned him. He wasn't sure where to go from here. He hurt. She hurt him.

"Toni hasn't been home since your little argument," he said derisively. "If you'd quit feeling so sorry for yourself you might have noticed that fact."

Simon glared at his friend. But a twinge of concern tightened his chest. He swore softly. He didn't want to feel concern. She was a big girl. She could take care of herself.

He didn't want to think about the phone call and how much courage it had taken for her to call him. He'd shoved it back in her face.

Matt looked up from his perch on the bench in front of the lockers. "She's still not home?"

A.J. all but snarled, surprising Simon with his ferocity. "I can't believe you, Matt. What's Toni done to you? This has nothing to do with you. Don't you give a crap that she's been gone for two days?"

"I'm a little pissed at her," Matt muttered.

"Well, get over it," A.J. growled. "Right now I'd say it's more important to find out where the hell she is. A freaking ice storm is supposed to hit, and we don't know if she's out on the road somewhere or what."

Simon's stomach clenched. Despite his anger, the thought of Toni out alone somewhere, hurt or scared, frightened the hell out of him. And their child. Christ. His child.

"You'll excuse my interruption, but you guys are complete dumbasses," Mike said as he rounded the corner. His eyes glittered angrily as he stared them down.

"Back off, Sanders," Simon said menacingly. "You don't have a clue what you're talking about."

"Don't I? Let's see. You're *not* sulking because Toni didn't tell you she was pregnant with your child, and you're not sulking because your little pride is hurt," he said sarcastically.

"What do you know about the situation?" Matt demanded, standing to his full height.

"I know you people are pathetic," he sneered. "Did I hear you right, A.J.? Is Toni missing?"

A.J. shrugged. "I wish I knew. She's not answering her phone, and this is the second day she's missed work."

"How is it you know so much about Toni's situation?" Simon asked, his voice deceptively soft. He was working to keep a tight rein on his anger, and Sander's smug expression was wearing his patience thin.

"You're an idiot, Simon. She is so in love with you it isn't even funny. She's agonized for months over how to tell you. Wondering if you'd hate her. Worried that if she told you, she'd never know if you really loved her or hooked up with her just for the baby."

"That's no excuse," he began, though his argument sounded hollow even to his own ears.

"I see, and what was she supposed to tell you, Simon? That on the night you broke up with your girlfriend, you stumbled home to Toni and took comfort in her arms? That after you took her virginity you humiliated her by calling her Starla? Somehow I don't see her lining up to admit what happened."

Simon felt the color drain from his face then close behind, a dull flush worked its way over his cheeks. "How do you know this? Did she tell you this?" Christ, had he really called her Starla?

"Uh, no, Simon. I was in the bedroom while you two made it." His heavy sarcasm was enough.

Simon bolted over and grabbed Mike by the collar, slamming him against the locker. "Shut the hell up, Sanders. I don't know why Toni confided in you, but shut your filthy mouth up."

"Could it be she had no one else?" Mike asked pointedly, not at all intimidated by Simon's strangle hold on him.

Simon slowly released him and he slid down the locker.

"You're a damn fool, Simon. I bet you've spent the last few months secretly wishing the baby was yours so you and Toni could be one big happy family. And now that your wish has been granted, you're doing your best to screw it up. Makes a hell of a lot of sense."

"As much as I hate to agree with pretty boy Sanders, he has a very good point," A.J. spoke up.

Simon turned to glare at A.J. who was leaning casually against the locker, anger still written on his face.

"Really, Simon. What's your problem? Don't you have everything you ever wanted? Didn't you say the other night that things would be such much simpler if it were your baby she carried?" A.J. asked.

"She should have told me," Simon whispered. "I had the right to know."

"Yeah well I don't think anyone's going to argue that with you. But it's a moot point. So are you going to hold it against her forever, or are you going to take care of the girl who loves you and raise your child together?" Mike stood defiantly a few inches from Simon's face as he laid down the challenge. "Personally, I don't think you deserve her, but for whatever reason, she chose you. She's never betrayed you, never even looked at another guy. How many women can you say that about? Certainly no one in your past," he said derisively.

"Enough already," Matt said, holding up a hand and inserting himself between Simon and Mike. "We've got work to do. Toni's a smart girl. She's probably off working this out on her own like Simon's doing. Back off and leave them to it."

"You screw this up, Simon, and I'll make damn sure you don't get another chance with her," Mike said as he stalked off.

Simon pounded his fist into the locker. "Damn it!" he swore. He turned to A.J. "You think I'm a jerk don't you?"

"Well...not in so many words. I have a feeling you were pretty harsh on her though. Maybe said some things you shouldn't have."

"Tell me about it," he muttered, thinking back to her earlier phone call. *We have nothing to talk about* rang in his ears. He looked back up at A.J. "She hasn't been home in two days?"

A.J. shook his head. "Not that I've seen. I've called several times and I've driven by a few times."

"She called me earlier today," he said in a low voice.

"She did? What did she say? Where was she?"

He flushed again, his guilt in major overdrive. "I don't know," he said lamely.

"You don't know?" Matt asked, finally speaking up.

"I hung up on her…after I told her we had nothing to talk about."

"Damn," A.J. said with a shake of his head. "You sure know how to put the screws to a person."

"Let's not haul me over the rack yet. I need to find out where she is. I'll call her from inside."

"If she'll talk to you now," A.J. said, raising one eyebrow.

Simon walked back inside and went straight to the phone. He dialed Toni's number and let it ring twenty some odd times. In frustration he hung up. Was A.J. right? Had she not been home in two days? It wasn't like her to miss so much work.

He picked up the phone and called the vet's office. After speaking to Marnie for a few minutes, he hung up, worry beginning to crawl up his spine.

"That was Marnie," he said as A.J. walked up behind him. "She's worried about Toni too. Said she called yesterday and it sounded like she was at a payphone somewhere. This morning she called and the connection was clearer but she didn't say anything other than she was sick and not coming in."

A.J. frowned. "Doesn't sound good, man."

The radio went off and the crew launched into action. Simon swore and pulled his gear on. According to the scanner, the ice was already starting to build on the secondary roads. It was only a matter of time before the main roads started to freeze as well.

Leave it to Mother Nature to pull a freak ice storm in southeast Texas in December. He'd be lucky if he had time to call Toni again. Traffic accidents would mount as the ice formed. People in these parts had no idea how to drive in this kind of weather.

"Let's go," the chief shouted.

Simon pulled on his helmet and climbed into the truck. It was going to be a long day. His worry over Toni wasn't going to make it any easier. His own nagging guilt was merely another nail in his coffin.

🚌 🚌 🚌

As Toni drove the lonely stretch of highway between Beaumont and Cypress, she thought, not for the first time, that she would have been better off remaining in her hotel room on the coast. While the sleet was coming down along the coastal rode, it wasn't sticking. But here, just miles north, the roads were quickly icing over.

"Whoever heard of an ice storm in December?" she grumbled. She slowed to a crawl as she crossed the bridge over Cypress creek. Only ten more miles and she'd be home. At an absurd hour of the night. Or morning, she thought as she checked her watch. It was almost two a.m.

She'd slept most of the day, her exhaustion extreme after a night up and the emotional turmoil she'd suffered before. She rubbed her belly as she slowed for another corner. "It's just you and me, kid. But I love you," she whispered. "And I don't regret anything."

Tears welled in her eyes again, stinging her eyelids. How much could she cry in a twenty-four hour period? She scrubbed at her face with the back of her hand.

When she pulled her hand away, she was suddenly blinded by a set of headlights. They were coming right for her. Too late, she realized the other vehicle was skidding out of control.

She gripped the steering wheel and yanked it over, trying desperately to avoid the oncoming car. With a sickening crunch, the car hit her broadside on the passenger side. The Jeep spun and lurched off the road. Her world turned upside down as the Jeep rolled. Pain exploded in her consciousness just before she registered a blast of cold air.

Chapter Twenty-Four

"Where are you, Toni?" Simon murmured as he dropped the phone beside the bed. He leaned back on the small cot and stared up at the ceiling. He'd done a lot of thinking today. Rational thinking. And he'd gained a unique perspective.

After he'd calmed down and separated through his feelings of hurt and betrayal, he'd immediately wanted to kick himself in the ass. Yeah, Toni had done the wrong thing in keeping the truth about her pregnancy from him, but if that was the worst thing she ever did he was one lucky guy.

And A.J. was right. He should be jumping for joy. He had gotten precisely what he'd spent the last month wishing for. The baby was his. Toni was his. There was no other guy in the picture.

He'd been her first. An inexplicable wave of satisfaction gripped him. But then he'd turned around and called her Starla. He could only imagine how that had made her feel.

He rubbed his eyes tiredly. It all made sense to him now. What he'd thought were vivid fantasies about her were actually snippets of memory from the night they had made love. Even now if he thought hard about the night in question, he could form hasty images of her. Naked beneath him. How good she'd felt. And he could remember kissing her. That much he knew wasn't a fantasy.

"Still can't sleep?" A.J. asked from across the room.

"Nah. Too busy kicking my ass. And I'm worried about Toni," he admitted.

A.J. got up and ambled over. He parked it in a chair next to Simon's cot. "She'll come around. She's probably just upset and taking a break."

"I was a jerk. She didn't deserve to be treated like I treated her. No matter how angry I was, she *is* pregnant with my child. The upset can't be good for either of them."

"Has it sunk in yet?" A.J. asked.

"That the baby is mine?"

A.J. nodded.

"It's the weirdest feeling. I can't even describe it. I mean I already felt extremely possessive of Toni. Some archaic cave man response. She's *mine*. Hands off. That sort of thing. But now it's even stronger. She's carrying my child. *Mine*. Her belly is swelling with a part of me. I can't get over it."

He looked down at his hands then back up at A.J. "Why didn't she just tell me? I think that's what I'm having the hardest time with. Toni had to know I'd take care of her. For that matter, why didn't she tell me what happened the next day? I could have been there for her when she first found out she was pregnant."

"Try to put yourself in her shoes," A.J. said softly. "You called her Starla. In her eyes that meant you were seriously hung up on your girlfriend. Not to mention it had to be pretty humiliating that you didn't even know it was her. And since she didn't tell you right away, when she found out she was pregnant, she probably thought you wouldn't believe her."

"And maybe I wouldn't have," Simon said honestly. "I don't know. I would have been shocked as hell, no doubt."

"She's been paying for her mistake," A.J. pointed out. "I'm sure this whole pregnancy has been less than a cakewalk for her. I'm sure she's been terrified the whole time that you would hate her. It can't have been easy living with that kind of fear and anxiety."

"You're right," Simon admitted.

The radio blared an alarm, and the chief shot out of bed, grabbing for his radio. Simon and A.J. strained to hear as the chief radioed ten-four.

"Let's roll, guys," Chief Maxwell said, heading for the locker room to grab his gear.

"What's up, chief?" A.J. asked as the rest rolled out of bed and dashed for the locker room.

"Two car MVA out on old Bridge Road a few miles out of town. They need extrication. One of the drivers is pinned inside the vehicle."

"Damn," Simon muttered.

"Why don't people stay the hell at home?" Mike grumbled. "It's two friggin' AM, and the roads are icy. Most people would have the sense not to drive."

"It gets better," the chief said, as they scrambled into the truck. "Ambulance is still twenty miles out and slow going in the ice. Their back up unit is in Beaumont."

"Make sure our medical supplies are handy," A.J. called out as he hopped on the truck.

They headed out onto the ice slickened street, the heavy fire truck faring better than lighter vehicles. They were probably a good five miles from the accident scene, and Simon hoped to hell the injuries to the driver weren't severe. He knew basic first aid, but he had no desire to play paramedic.

"Do we have an ETA on the ambulance yet?" he asked the chief.

"Still several miles out. The first responders said the driver trapped in the vehicle is unconscious and they can't get close enough to offer any assistance. We'll have to cut him out."

Simon nodded grimly and said a prayer that wherever Toni was, she stayed put.

As they neared the accident scene, flashing lights lit up the wooded area on both sides of the road. At least four first responder trucks were parked on the shoulder and the road had been closed off.

To the right, a Ford Expedition sat on the shoulder of the road, the front end completely caved in. Whatever they'd hit, they'd hit hard.

Simon hopped out with the other guys and was immediately met by Frank Parker, one of the first responders. "Are Matt and A.J. with you?" he asked, a peculiar expression on his face.

"Yeah, why?"

"You and A.J. are sidelined," Chief Maxwell said as he walked up. He pushed Simon back toward the truck and yelled for A.J. "Someone find out where the hell Matt went and get him in the truck," he directed one of the first responders.

"What the hell is going on?" Simon demanded. "You can't sideline us. We have an extrication to do."

"Mike and I will handle it," the chief said. "You get in the truck and stay there."

There was something in Chief Maxwell's eyes he didn't like. Sympathy and a bit of fear. Simon's stomach clenched. Before anyone could stop him, he shoved by Chief Maxwell and ran toward the embankment where a crowd of first responders, sheriff's deputies and the highway patrol stood.

A flash of yellow caught his eye. A cold sweat broke out on his forehead. Nausea rolled in his stomach, and he feared puking right there on the road.

He shoved forward, not wanting to believe what his eyes were telling him. It wasn't Toni's Jeep. It couldn't be. It was another yellow Jeep. It had to be.

His heart was jamming double time as he shoved aside the people gathered. Someone tried to pull him back, but he came up swinging. Maybe he connected, he wasn't sure, but his knuckles hurt like hell.

He slid down the ravine, his feet not cooperating with his brain. He came to a stop beside two men from his crew who were setting up cables from the wench so they could pull the Jeep right side up.

Dropping down on his belly, he slithered forward, yanking his flashlight from his belt and shining it into the interior of the Jeep. His heart nearly stopped when he caught sight of Toni's blood covered face. "Get me some light down here!" he yelled back up.

A.J. came sliding down seconds later carrying a floodlight. He tossed it to one of the first responders and directed him to hold it up.

"Damn it, you two," the chief yelled as he scrambled down the embankment. "I don't need a bunch of half-cocked firemen out of their heads with worry. Get back. We'll get her out."

Simon ignored him completely, his focus on Toni, trying to see if she was breathing. A.J. argued fiercely above him, and apparently he was successful because he bent down and pointed his own flashlight into the interior of the Jeep.

It was one giant cluster. The Jeep had come to rest against a tree, almost completely turned over. Toni leaned heavily against her door, and blood dripped down her forehead. Simon shoved himself closer to her, reaching for her neck. Gently so as not to compromise her spine, he pressed his fingers into her flesh, praying desperately that he found a pulse.

Sweet relief poured over him. She was alive. For now. He shined the light down her body, grimly noting her legs trapped under the smashed in dash and steering wheel. Her left arm was fixed in an unnatural angle, obviously broken. Her rounded abdomen rested against the steering wheel, and he wondered how much of a blow her belly took.

"Where are the damn paramedics?" he shouted hoarsely.

"They're three minutes out," A.J. said, his voice filled with anxiety.

Simon swore and turned his attention back to Toni. "Toni, Toni, sweetheart. Can you hear me? It's me, Simon. Wake up, baby."

He reached a hand out to touch her cheek, wiping the blood away as more ran down. God, he couldn't lose her now. He hadn't gotten to tell her how sorry he was, and how much he loved her. "Don't take her from me," he whispered fiercely, hoping the words wrenched from the depths of his soul somehow made it to God's ears.

Matt picked that moment to career down the incline, despite the responders' best attempts to hold him back. He got down with Simon. "How does it look?" His voice was sick with worry.

"Is there anything I can do?" A.J. asked desperately.

Simon shook his head. "Are they through with the cables yet? We've got to get the Jeep turned over so we can get her out of here."

"Get back," the chief barked. "We're going to try and get the vehicle back on its wheels."

Reluctantly Simon eased back, his heart in turmoil. What if they couldn't save her? He knew every minute she stayed trapped in the Jeep, the less chance she had of surviving. The golden rule of emergencies. Get the patient to the hospital as fast as you can.

The Jeep shook and the steel cables creaked in protest as they began reeling them in. After a groan, the Jeep swayed up and down. Then in one loud bang, it righted itself, landing heavily on the ground.

"Damn it, that was too rough!" Simon swore, rushing forward.

"We'll have to cut the dash," A.J. said as he, Matt and Simon surrounded Toni.

"Move away," a new voice demanded.

Simon turned to see a paramedic, jump bag in hand, pushing him aside.

"It's about damn time," he growled.

"Get back and let me do my job," he said in an even tone. He looked over at A.J. and Matt. "Look, I know this is tough for you guys, but back off."

Simon moved a foot back, unwilling to get too far away from Toni. The paramedic slipped a C-collar around her neck then checked her lungs. He cast a cursory glance over her broken arm then began prepping the other one for an IV as another paramedic rushed up with an oxygen bottle.

"I'll hold it," Simon offered, when the paramedic couldn't get the mask to stay.

He nodded, and Simon stepped forward, holding the rebreather over her mouth and nose.

The Jeep shook and the loud noise of the jaws rent the night air as Mike and the chief began cutting into the dash to free her legs.

In a few minutes, the dash was peeled away, and the paramedic shouted for the stretcher. After a few minutes of securing her spine, they began the slow process of lifting her from the jeep and laying her on the stretcher.

Several hands helped lug the stretcher up the steep drop off, and once they reached the road, the paramedic picked up the pace, racing over to the ambulance.

"You can ride if you stay out of my way," he said bluntly, as Simon arrived at the back of the ambulance.

Simon nodded and climbed in.

"We'll meet you at the hospital," Matt called.

The doors slammed shut, and the ambulance started forward, as fast as conditions would allow.

Simon glanced down at Toni's bloodied face. His heart constricted. There was so much blood. And the baby. How was the baby?

"Here," the paramedic said, handing him a bottle of saline and a wad of bandages. "Get her face cleaned off so I can assess the damage.

Simon took the bottle and gently began wiping at her face. He could see no sign of trauma to her forehead or nose. Which meant she had sustained an injury to her scalp somewhere. He steadied his hand, not allowing his fear to overwhelm him. He couldn't see a head injury for her hair, but the blood was coming from somewhere.

The paramedic's fingers probed through her hair, pulling it away and shining a light on her scalp.

Simon winced when they came across a large gash in the top of her head. He lost view of it when the paramedic bent over it to examine it further. How deep had it gone?

"What's your assessment?" he asked, no longer able to wait.

"Her vitals are okay. A bit weak, but it's probably from the blood loss. Her pressure is stable right now, but depending on the extent of the head injury, that could change any time."

"And the baby?" he asked fearfully.

The paramedic looked up at him, sympathy bright in his eyes. "I don't know, man. I don't have the equipment needed to make that assessment. Her legs are good considering the dash was crushed around them. I didn't detect any breaks. Just some bruising. Her arm's broken, but her breath sounds are good, so hopefully that means there's no broken ribs or lung involvement."

Simon allowed himself a small breath of relief. It could have been a lot worse, although all it took was one head injury and she could be taken from him.

The ride to the hospital was the longest of his life. He stroked Toni's face, willing her to wake up. He spent the rest of the time beating himself up. She wouldn't be in this situation if he hadn't been such an ass.

She'd be home with him, in bed, in his arms. She'd have his ring on her finger, and they'd be planning a wedding. Picking out baby names.

God. He couldn't bear to imagine that scenario not taking place. More than anything he wanted to spend the rest of his life with her. Even at his angriest, he'd never contemplated being without her. He'd wanted to punish her. Make her feel all the hurt he'd felt. Only now, she was fighting for her life because of his stupidity.

When they finally pulled up at the hospital, she was quickly wheeled into the exam room. Two doctors and a host of nurses immediately went to work. Orders for x-rays were shouted. Cat scan, blood work, O2 sat. Monitors were hooked up. Another IV was started.

He watched from the door as the flurry of activity increased. No one tried to make him leave. Perhaps they saw the futility in it. He wasn't moving.

Finally, the most blessed sound he'd ever heard in his life filtered over the noise of the room. Toni moaned softly. But he heard it. He pushed a nurse aside and ran to the head of the bed.

The nurse started to protest, but the doctor shook his head.

"Toni? Toni? Can you hear me?" he demanded.

A doctor peeled her eyelids back and checked her pupils. She winced and blinked rapidly as her eyes fluttered open. She immediately shut her eyes again, her face going white with pain.

"What's wrong?" Simon demanded, looking frantically at the doctor.

"She's fine," the doctor soothed. "Our main concerns right now are the extent of her head injury and the baby."

The baby. He'd forgotten all about their child.

"We're going to hook up a monitor. I've paged the OB on call, and he's on his way in. Right now, we've got to get her to CT so we can rule out any subcranial bleeding."

Simon allowed himself to breathe.

"Why don't you wait outside?" the nurse gently prompted. "We're sending her to CT, but as soon as she's back, I'll call you."

Reluctantly, he backed from the room, his eyes never leaving her beautiful face. As he walked into the waiting room, A.J. and Matt leaped from their chairs. "How is she?" Matt asked, his voice strained. A.J.'s face was a mask of worry, his eyes tense as he waited for Simon to speak.

"I don't really know," he admitted. "They're still doing tests. I mean, the doctor thought she would be fine, but they still have to do a CT scan because of her head injury, and they have to check out the baby...our baby," he added softly.

He felt A.J.'s hand on his shoulder. It was the last straw. Harsh, guttural sobs spilled forth, shocking himself with the agonized sound that ripped from his throat. He sank down in a chair, his body shaking, as tears ran freely down his face.

Matt and A.J. took a seat on either side of him, but remained quiet as he buried his face in his hands. As they sat there waiting, more firemen filtered in as the men who had been on duty for the accident got off work. The ambulance personnel from the night before along with members of dispatch, first responders and sheriff's deputies stood in the now crowded waiting room, all waiting for word of Toni.

She was loved by a lot of people, but none more than Simon. She had taken hold of his heart. Firmly entrenched herself into his life, and he couldn't imagine being without her.

If it took the rest of his life, he was going to make it up to her for the careless words he'd thrown at her. *We have nothing to talk about.*

Chapter Twenty-Five

Simon was about to go out of his mind when a nurse opened the door and motioned for him to follow her back. Matt rose as well, and the nurse smiled at him. "I'm sorry, but for now, I can only allow one person back."

Matt looked as though he would argue for a moment, and Simon felt a brief moment of fear. Technically Matt was more entitled than he was to be with Toni. Matt was her brother, while he was, well, not much. But being the baby's father counted for something.

He looked over at Matt, and Matt nodded before taking his seat again. "Thanks man," Simon said quietly.

He followed the nurse back to the exam room, shocked to see the amount of lines, wires and bandages that surrounded Toni. Her head was wrapped in gauze, and her arm still had the ladder splint the paramedic had used to stabilize the break.

They had removed the oxygen mask, which to Simon meant serious cause for relief. Her head injury must not be severe. As he walked over, she blinked and unfocused eyes swept past him and around the room. Her lips worked up and down as if she were trying desperately to speak.

He rushed to her side and put his fingers to her cheek. "Toni, sweetheart, it's Simon."

Her brown eyes settled on him a split second before utter hurt swamped their depths. She looked away, tears brimming around her eyelids.

He started to ask if she was in pain, but he knew the anguish he saw had nothing to do with physical discomfort. He wanted to pour out his heart, beg her forgiveness, but the nurse had been very explicit in her instructions not to upset or overtire her.

Instead he curled his fingers around her uninjured hand and hoped he could speak volumes with his touch.

Toni turned away from Simon, the pain she felt at his presence far superseding the pain that racked her body. She felt his hand curl around hers, and comforting warmth snaked up her arm. She was afraid. So afraid. And of course he would be here. She was pregnant with his baby after all.

She closed her eyes willing the baby to move within her, needing to feel the stirring of life within her. The on call obstetrician had visited her a few minutes ago, checking her cervix for dilation and listening for the baby's heartbeat.

The heartbeat had been strong much to her relief, but she had yet to feel it move within her womb. The doctor had explained that after a shock, it wasn't uncommon for the baby to be still for a longer period of time. He felt confident the baby was fine, but he ordered a monitor hooked up so they could make sure she wasn't contracting.

Her head hurt, her arm hurt, her legs hurt, her *heart* hurt. She struggled to remember the chain of events that left her lying in the emergency room. She vaguely remembered another car, blinding headlights and overwhelming pain and fear. And then Simon, begging her not to leave him. Commanding her to wake up. Had she dreamed all that?

She chanced another glimpse of Simon who still stood rigidly by her bed. He looked back at her, concern flaring in his eyes. And something else. Was it fear?

She looked away, no longer able to meet his eyes. Her shame was too great. He had every right to be angry with her. His words—the last words he'd spoken to her—rang in her ears. Yet he was here. Did she want to know why? Yes. Yes, she did.

She raised her eyes once more to meet his and opened her mouth to speak. Her throat felt funny, and her tongue wouldn't cooperate at all. She tried again, and Simon put a finger over her lips. "Shh, sweetheart. Don't try to talk right now. Just rest. I'll be here when you wake up I promise."

She felt oddly comforted by his statement, and for a minute, she could forget he despised her. Her eyes flickered to the doorway as she saw it open. A.J. peeked his head through then walked in, followed closely by Matt.

"We only have a minute," A.J. said as Simon stared questioningly at them. She glanced between them, her head hurting from the effort. "They're about to move her to the floor."

A.J. walked to her bedside, and Simon moved back out of the way. He bent over and kissed her softly on the forehead. "You scared us, girl. Don't ever do that again." He attempted to tease her, but she could hear the stark fear in his voice.

Matt stood at the foot of her bed looking guilty. Her brow furrowed as she watched him fidget, his eyes full of regret. "I'm sorry, Toni," he said in a tortured voice. "I should have been there. I was an ass. A complete jerk for being mad at you."

Confusion filled her mind. What was he talking about? Why was he mad at her? Her head began to pound all over again. She looked at Simon then back at Matt. Matt was angry with her. It was more than she could stand at the moment. Faced with losing the man she loved and her best friend to boot, having her big brother pissed at her was the straw that broke the camel's back.

Tears filled her eyes and she tried hard to speak. To say something. That she was sorry. But nothing came out. A.J. looked angry, and Matt looked more contrite than ever. The nurse pushed her way into the door and quickly ordered them all out. Simon lingered until the nurse took his arm and all but dragged him from the room. "We've got to cast her arm then we're transferring her to the floor. You can see her later," she said firmly.

Toni watched them go then slumped wearily against her pillow. The doctor came in with a clipboard and stood a few feet from her as the nurse began swabbing her arm. "You're a lucky young lady," he said, eyeing her over his glasses.

She swallowed hard and tried once more to find her tongue. "W-when can I go home?" she rasped. Her free hand came to her throat and massaged absently.

He laughed. "Go home? You're in an awful big hurry. You won't be going home for a few days. I want to keep an eye on that head injury of yours.

And your obstetrician wants to monitor the baby. Make sure the little tyke stays put. We're going to give you a fiberglass cast. Nurse McGregor will give you your post release care instructions, but the floor nurse will run through it all again before you're released. Do you have any questions?"

"I hurt," she croaked.

He gave her a sympathetic look. "Your OB left orders as to what you could have. I defer to him on matters of pregnancy. I'll make sure you're given something before you leave the ER."

"Thank you," she managed. The effort of speaking was overwhelming, and she closed her eyes, exhausted.

The nurse's ministrations barely registered, though she winced when her arm was set. She was given an injection of pain medication, and soon she floated in a sea of painlessness.

She vaguely held a sensation of moving, the blurry walls of the hallways passing by her. She saw Simon's head bob in front of her view then fade away as her eyes grew heavy.

🚌 🚌 🚌

She opened her eyes, and at first, she had no idea where she was. It wasn't as bright as the emergency room had been, the dark soothing to her aching head. As her vision cleared, she could see she was in a private room.

As she scanned the room, her eyes came to rest on the chair next to her bed where Simon slouched, asleep, his head lolled to the side. She drank in the sight of him. His dark hair fell forward over his forehead. Dark shadows left imprints under his eyes. He looked as bad as she felt, but he'd never looked more desirable to her.

She tested her arm, waiting for the flash of pain when she lifted it up to inspect the cast. To her relief, all she felt was mild discomfort.

She reached up with her unencumbered hand and felt the bandages on her head. The doctor had explained to her she'd suffered a large laceration to her scalp that required multiple stitches, but thankfully it hadn't resulted in a serious head injury.

She allowed her hand to fall back to her chest then she slid it down over her belly. She rubbed in a circle, sending a mental apology to her unborn baby. When her belly shifted and fluttered under her fingers, she gasped, tears flooding to her eyes.

Simon came awake immediately, lurching to his feet and coming to her side. "What is it? What's wrong?" he demanded.

"N-nothing," she stammered, relieved she wasn't as hoarse now. "I was worried about the baby and she just moved." Tears slipped down her cheeks unchecked.

His reached his hand out and smoothed it over her belly. His touch comforted her in a way no medication could. Warmth burned through her where his hand soothed. "So he or she is okay," he said, relief evident in his voice.

"The doctor says so," she said lamely.

A knock sounded at the door, and Simon raised his head, an irritated expression on his face.

A.J. walked in ahead of Matt and Stephanie, his face lighting up when he saw Toni. "You're awake."

She swallowed. "You act surprised."

He bent down and kissed her cheek. "Hell yeah. You slept all day and all night."

She frowned. "You mean it's tomorrow?"

He laughed. "Yeah, you've been asleep over eighteen hours."

"She needed the rest," Simon said grumpily. "What are you guys doing here? I told you I'd call when she woke up."

"I see you did just that," Matt said with a raised eyebrow. He leaned over and kissed Toni on top of the head. Stephanie stood anxiously beside him, her worried gaze on Toni.

"How are you doing, Toni?" she asked.

"I didn't call because she only just woke up," Simon replied.

"I'm okay," Toni said in answer to Stephanie's question. She tried a convincing smile, but it made her head ache so she dropped the effort.

"We were worried about you," Matt said, staring intently at her. "You shouldn't have been out on the roads."

Heat crept into her cheeks.

"Shut the hell up, Matt," Simon growled. "She doesn't need a lecture right now. We all know whose fault it was she was out there."

Toni froze, his words cutting deeply into her. He couldn't have said any clearer that he blamed her for the accident. She bit her lip, wishing she could sink back into oblivion. It didn't hurt so badly when she was asleep.

"Why don't the two of you go take a hike?" A.J. said evenly. "I want to talk to Toni, and the two of you are only upsetting her."

Stephanie frowned. "A very good idea," she said fiercely. She hooked her arm through Simon's and all but dragged him and Matt toward the door.

A.J. shot her an apologetic look and pulled Simon's chair up to the bed. He sat down and picked up her hand. "Nice cast," he said, eyeing her other arm.

She smiled shakily, tried to speak, but burst into tears instead.

"Aww hell, Toni. Don't cry. You know I'm worthless when it comes to tears." He smudged at the damp trails with his thumb. "Are you okay? Do I need to call the nurse? If you keep crying, the two lug nuts are going to come charging back in here, and I'll be forced to punch their headlights out."

She tried to smile but only succeeded in crying harder. A.J. sat quietly, waiting for her to stop. He didn't fuss over here, which was refreshing. But then he'd always given her the most breathing room. He stroked her hand until her sobs subsided.

"Better?" he asked.

She nodded. "Thanks," she choked out.

"Do you need anything?" he asked.

"Not unless you can take me back a few months and let me do things all over again," she said painfully.

"You did the best you could," he said quietly.

"Will you stay?" she asked, begging him with her eyes.

He looked confused. "Sure, I'll hang out for awhile."

"No, I mean will you stay. I don't want...I don't want to stay by myself," she finished.

His brow furrowed. "Ah, sure. I mean okay, if that's what you want." He scratched his head, clearly baffled by her request. Perhaps he imagined Simon would be staying, but she couldn't bear his scrutiny. His solicitous attention. It was too easy for her to think he cared.

"I shouldn't have asked," she mumbled. Her request obviously discomfited him.

"I said I'll stay," he said firmly. "When are they letting you out anyway?"

"I don't know," she said truthfully. "The ER doc said a few days, but that was yesterday. So maybe tomorrow?"

"I don't see them letting you go that quick," he said with a frown. "You look like hell."

"Gee thanks," she muttered. "I can always count on you to be honest."

He smiled at her. "I'm going to go get the lugs before they wear a hole in the floor."

He paused as she looked at him in panic. He must have read the fear in her eyes, because he squeezed her hand. "I told you I'd stay."

A.J. stepped into the hall, and Simon immediately started from the door. A.J.'s arm caught him. "Maybe you should go home for awhile, man," he said quietly.

Confusion then anger surged in his blood. "I'm not leaving her," he insisted, angry that A.J. would even suggest it.

A.J. sighed as Matt and Stephanie joined them. "Look, I know how you feel, Simon. I don't blame you, but she is walking a fine line in there. One minute she's looking like the weight of the world's on her shoulders, and the next she's sobbing her heart out."

"She's upset?" Simon demanded, his heart lurching at the thought of her crying.

"Let me finish," A.J. interjected. "She's been through a hell of an ordeal, and I'm not trying to make you feel bad, Simon, but her emotions are raw. I don't think now is the time to hash it out between you. Let her rest. Heal. She needs it. You have all the time in the world to make it right. Just give her time."

Simon looked away and swore. A.J. was right, but damn it, he didn't want to leave her. He'd almost lost her, and he couldn't stand the thought of being away from her for even a minute.

"I don't think she should stay alone," Matt spoke up.

"She's not," A.J. said. "She asked me to stay with her."

Simon's hands curled into fists at his side. "She doesn't want me to stay?"

"I didn't say that," A.J. said calmly. "If I had to guess, she doesn't even imagine you want to stay."

"Which is why I need to be here," he persisted. "I won't allow her to continue believing the horrible things I said to her."

"Not now," Stephanie said firmly, stepping forward, her eyes flashing.

Simon stepped back in surprise. Matt looked no less shocked.

"You two aren't helping with your guilt complexes," she said scornfully. She rounded on Matt. "I can't believe you, mister." She stabbed her finger into his chest. "Taking sides against your own sister. And you," she said, whirling on Simon, "I don't even have words for you. This isn't about you and absolving yourself of the awful guilt you're feeling. If you're miserable that's too bad. But Toni doesn't need this right now. She's injured and she's pregnant, and frankly, she needs the two of you hanging around like she needs a hole in the head."

She stood with her hands on her hips, her breath coming out in a huff.

A.J. laughed. "I knew there was a reason I liked her so much," he drawled. "Couldn't have said it better myself."

"You make sure she gets rest," she ordered, glaring A.J. down.

Simon frowned. Stephanie was right. It pained him to admit it, and it would kill him to put off pouring out his heart to Toni. But she was right. It wasn't the time. The most important thing was for Toni to get well. Then he'd bring her home. To their home.

Chapter Twenty-Six

Simon paced restlessly outside Toni's room three days later. The nurse was in the process of discharging her, and he was going to take her home. A.J. had stayed with her the entire time as he'd promised her he would. As grateful as he was to A.J. for providing much needed support, he resented the fact that he hadn't been the one she leaned on.

But he only had himself to blame.

The door cracked open and he heard voices inside. "Do you want to walk or do you want me to get a wheelchair?" the nurse asked.

"I'll walk." Toni's soft voice filtered through the door. She still sounded weak.

He strode in the room, unable to stay away from her a moment longer. She reacted in surprise, leaning against the bed where she stood. "I thought A.J. was coming," she said in a shaky voice.

"I'm taking you home," he said firmly.

Uncertainty flashed in her eyes.

"Are you ready?" the nurse asked gently.

Toni nodded, and Simon wrapped an arm around her shoulders. He could feel her shaking and he tightened his hold on her. She felt unbelievably fragile, like she would break into a million pieces with the slightest touch.

He shepherded her down the hall and punched the button for the elevator. She'd dressed in a loose fitting shirt and sweat pants. He frowned when he realized he had forgotten to bring her a coat. Thankfully, he'd parked under the awning at the front entrance, and he'd left the heat running.

They walked slowly through the lobby, and as the door slid open automatically, cold air blew over them. She shivered, and he hurried her around to the passenger side. After she was belted in, he closed the door and walked around to the driver's side.

He drove away, chewing on the inside of his lip. Everything rode on today. He'd planned meticulously, covering every angle, but the difficult part lay ahead. Convincing her to forgive him and give him another chance.

Toni stared out the window, glad to be going home, but surprised Simon had been the one to collect her. A.J. had left saying he'd return to pick her up when she was discharged. Had something come up?

To her surprise, they drove past her road. She turned to look at him. "Where are we going?"

"It's a surprise," he said, glancing over her.

She sat back, not sure what to say in response. Surprise? The only surprise was that he was still speaking to her. Maybe the guys were waiting for her at the house. A welcome home party of sorts.

But then he turned into the driveway of a house a block down from the guys' house.

"Why are we here?" she asked.

"I'll tell you in a minute," he said as he got out. He came around and helped her down, keeping a strong arm around her.

He unlocked the door and swung it open. She glanced around the empty house in total confusion. The house had been vacated for months, the previous owners transferred to Dallas. The house had been on the market nearly as long, but she didn't remember seeing the for sale sign when they'd driven up.

He took her right hand and pulled her tightly against his chest. His hand smoothed over her hair, mindful of her bandage. "I don't even know where to start, sweetheart."

Her chest tightened and she closed her eyes, enjoying his arms around her.

He pulled her away and looked intently into her eyes. "But let me start by saying I love you. I love you more than anything. And I am so sorry for the awful things I said. The terrible way I treated you."

His eyes shone with regret, pain reflected deeply in their depths.

"But—"

"No buts," he said, effectively shushing her with his lips. He kissed her gently, lingeringly.

"I was an ass. A first class jerk, and I don't deserve you. I'll never forgive myself for you being out on the road when you should have been safely at home waiting for me to come home to you."

"It wasn't your fault," she said softly. "I lied to you."

"Yes, you did," he said forthrightly. "But nothing you did was worth the way I responded. I took advantage of you, just as much as you took advantage of me. You were afraid. You should have never been in that position. I *put* you in that position," he said angrily.

She remained silent, not knowing how to respond to all he had said. Hope beat a steady rhythm in her chest, but she didn't dare give free rein to it yet.

"I brought you here because this is the house I was going to buy as a Christmas present," he said. "I planned to ask you to marry me the night you told me about the baby. I wanted to give you your dream. The perfect house. Perfect husband—or as perfect as I could be," he added with a grin. "Children, love, happiness. The whole shebang."

He blurred before her as tears sprang to her eyes. She wiped hastily at them not wanting to miss anything in his expression.

"I've put in an offer now because I want to marry you more than anything, Toni. I want to raise our children here. But most of all, I want to spend the rest of my life loving you."

She opened her mouth, but no words would come. She stared at him in shock. Wonder.

"Can you ever forgive me, Toni?" he asked softly, his eyes pleading with her.

"Oh my God," she cried, launching herself into his arms. She began to sob noisily as his arms wrapped around her like bands of steel. He held her tightly, his face buried in her neck. She could feel warm tears slide down her neck, and her heart clenched. God, how she loved this man.

"Yes, yes, yes!" she exclaimed. "I forgive you, and more than anything I want to marry you."

He caught her lips with his, kissing her breathlessly, passionately, as if he'd never let her go. She wrapped her arms around him and clunked him on the head with her cast. She let out a giggle. "Sorry."

He released her, his eyes roving over her possessively. "Be serious about this, Toni, because I'm never going to let you go. I've waited too long for you. I think I've loved you forever, but was too stubborn to see it."

She smiled up at him, her heart firmly in her eyes for him to see. "I love you too, Simon. So much."

"Want to see the house?" he asked, grinning down at her.

Her mouth rounded in shock. "Oh my God, you really did it didn't you?"

"We close in a month," he said. He dipped his head to hers once more. "Merry Christmas, sweetheart. I love you."

"I love you too," she whispered.

Between them the baby rolled and Simon's hand went to cup her belly. "I think our little urchin approves," he said softly.

Toni smiled. A deliriously happy smile. All the hurt of the past week was forgotten. She'd gotten her dream. Every single nuance of it. She was going to live every day of her life laughing and loving.

He tugged her along, his eyes bright with joy. She warmed all over. They were in their house. Home where they belonged. Together.

Maya Banks

Maya lives in Texas with her husband, three children and assortment of cats. When she's not writing, she can be found hunting, fishing or playing poker. A southern girl born and bred, Maya loves life below the Mason Dixon, and more importantly, loves bringing southern characters and settings to life in her stories.

To learn more about Maya, check out her website www.mayabanks.com or email Maya at maya@mayabanks.com.

Samhain Publishing, Ltd.

It's all about the story...

Action/Adventure
Fantasy
Historical
Horror
Mainstream
Mystery/Suspense
Non-Fiction
Paranormal
Red Hots!
Romance
Science Fiction
Western
Young Adult

http://www.samhainpublishing.com